JON THURLEY

THE ENIGMA VARIATIONS

VIKING

VIKING

Published by the Penguin Group
27 Wrights Lane, London w8 5TZ, England
Viking Penguin Inc., 40 West 23rd Street, New York, New York 10010, USA
Penguin Books Australia Ltd, Ringwood, Victoria, Australia
Penguin Books Canada Ltd, 2801 John Street, Markham, Ontario, Canada L3R 1B4
Penguin Books (NZ) Ltd, 182-190 Wairau Road, Auckland 10, New Zealand

Penguin Books Ltd, Registered Offices: Harmondsworth, Middlesex, England

First published 1988

Copyright © Jon Thurley, 1988

All rights reserved.
Without limiting the rights under copyright
reserved above, no part of this publication may be
reproduced, stored in or introduced into a retrieval system,
or transmitted, in any form or by any means (electronic, mechanical,
photocopying, recording or otherwise), without the prior
written permission of both the copyright owner and
the above publisher of this book

Filmset in Linotron 202 Bembo

Typeset, printed and bound in Great Britain by
Hazell Watson & Viney Limited
Member of BPCC plc
Aylesbury, Bucks, England

A CIP catalogue record for this book is available from the British Library

Library of Congress Catalog Card No.: 88-50733

ISBN 0-670-82148-9

It will work something like this. Some time in the near future – it may be next year, it may be five years – they'll announce they have an arms limitation deal. The press will hail Reagan and Gorbachev – or whoever happens to be in their positions at the time – as historic figures for having achieved this great step for mankind. But the main arsenals will remain untouched. Nothing will really have changed. Nobody gives anything away, really. It's all propaganda . . .
– unnamed White House source, May 1986

Nothing pleases a man so much as the downfall of his friends.
– La Rochefoucauld, *Maxims*

And be these juggling friends no more believed,
That palter with us in a double sense;
That keep the word of promise to our ear,
And break it to our hope!
– Shakespeare, *Macbeth*

PROLOGUE

Sir Joseph Sainsbury began to dress for the reception. Mrs Denton, his housekeeper, had left at five-thirty promptly. Getting some ice for his whisky from the fridge, Joseph had picked up the smell of her 'nice piece of haddock'. It was one of her many little habits which had persisted over the years, despite his mild protests. 'Go on, Sir Joseph. Nothing wrong with a little smell of good, healthy fish . . .'

Mrs Plunkett, his secretary, had been very slow in leaving, picking over her carbons, standing irresolutely at the filing cabinets. Finally, with seeming reluctance, she had left a good forty minutes past her usual time. Easing himself into his starched shirt and peering into the mirror while he fed the studs into the fly with clumsy fingers, he wondered if everything was all right at home. It was three years since she had suddenly burst into tears one Friday afternoon, bending her iron-grey head over the pad on her knee. Her crying lacked the appeal that pretty women sometimes had when they were upset. 'I'm sorry, I'm sorry,' she had said over and over, weeping ever more copiously each time she spoke. And Joseph, guilty that he had never suspected her distress, never thought of Mrs Plunkett even having a private life, said, haltingly, 'If it will help, tell me . . .'

It had been a twenty-year-old typist. Eve Plunkett had

gone back unexpectedly early – 'the day you told me to take the afternoon off and enjoy the park' – and there Julian had been, in bed with this kid young enough, almost, to be his granddaughter. 'How can I ever trust him again?' she asked, the tears trailing black mascara down her haggard face, and Joseph had said, gently, 'Is it so important in itself, then? When men's powers begin to fade they sometimes need reassurance. The mistake is to think that it has anything to do with love or permanence . . . ' After a while she had stopped crying, wiped her nose, even sipped the brandy he had put down on the table by her side. 'What should I do?' she asked, like a child, and he had said, 'Only you can say if it is worth setting aside your life for the past twenty years for this. That is, if this is all that has happened . . . ' He had deliberately avoided inviting further disclosures, ashamed at his own relief when she had said, only half convinced, 'I suppose not . . .' They had never referred to the occasion since, but he wondered sometimes, tonight, for example, if his advice then had been for the best. I'm from the darn-and-mend school, he thought, remembering suddenly his parents' quarrelling voices through the thin wall. Joseph sighed, undoing his tie to start refashioning it again. More and more of late he had found himself unexpectedly visited by an unwelcome compassion, a sudden insight into some quiet desperation he could not ignore.

In the street below, his chauffeur, Hastings, sounded the horn twice in the signal they had used over the years. Joseph, re-tying his bow for the third time, went to the window and pulled the curtain aside, holding up the fingers of his right hand twice. Ten minutes. The car lights flashed, and he went back to the mirror. It was how his life ran: order, the routine of each day, the careful consideration of each week ahead so that he could channel his resources most effectively. It was that order which had begun to feel threatened by some entropy, mirroring the slow dissolution of his body. And it had begun to seem that order no longer had the old, primal importance, might even be less important than giving his time to the Mrs Plunketts and their problems.

He had brushed his grey, crinkly hair back from his forehead. Long since he had stopped really looking at himself in the mirror. Even now, nearing seventy, he mourned the ugliness which he had tried over the years to combat with his wit, his attentiveness, his achievements. Concentrating on his hair, he avoided looking at the blunt, bulbous nose, the jowls, deckled with brown liver spots, which hung over his collar. Or, if his eyes wandered lower, the wide shirt front, under which years of rich living had bulged his stomach below heavy dugs covered in grey hair. In all those seventy years nothing had compensated him for this: the starred double first at Oxford, the firm of solicitors he had slowly built from one room in the Gray's Inn Road to their present luxurious premises in Park Lane, his directorships, or the charities to whom he gave his time so freely (to the concern of some of his younger partners). It was a tribute to his powers of deception that none of his friends and acquaintances were aware of the secret unhappiness he had nursed over the years; he expressed himself with such intelligence and good humour that people who met him soon forgot his appearance. It was a locked chamber in his soul which he had never revealed to anyone.

He and Elaine had no children. When she was dying, holding his hand in the ward at the Royal Marsden, with flowers all around and that faint, sweet odour of decay hanging in the air, she said, 'You didn't mind? Tell me really?' And he had squeezed her hand and said, 'Of course not,' watching the strained smile fade as she slipped into sleep again. Truly, he had not minded; he would have dreaded teaching a child to live with a legacy of ugliness, to know that it would be spurned, rejected, laughed at, always alone.

Only Andre Sheyrer, physician, friend, amiable rival since their Oxford days together, came near. 'Endogenous depression,' he said once, taking a brandy at the bar after bridge at the club. Quickly (too quickly, perhaps, seeing Andre's brief, speculative glance rest upon him) Joseph dissembled. He grumbled, with a deliberate lack of conviction, about his workload, about the Revenue's hard-hearted decision on some charity income, about growing old, always aware of Andre's barely visible smile. In the end, letting Andre into one of the secret chambers (though not the final one), he said, 'I feel uneasy. It's nothing tangible. I can't altogether trust this long peace, these rapprochements, this empty, material *plenty* which afflicts us now.' Andre had relaxed and, acting now, Joseph paused, and said, smiling, 'Perhaps that is depression. To fear the good life. To ask for meaning. To think of eternity . . . ' And, laughing together, they had gone on to talk more comfortably of the past, of other things.

The car horn sounded again. I'm getting forgetful, he thought, rising from his seat on the bed. At the door he paused to look around the sitting-room, as he always did, to check that the windows were closed against the rain, that Elaine's picture was standing on the mantelshelf. Walking down the stairs he felt again the sharp pain behind his breastbone. And again made a note to have a check-up.

At dinner Joseph was seated next to Ronald Atkins. It was no secret that Atkins was on the way down. One of Ronald's closest friends had said to Joseph, over a drink at the Garrick, 'The trouble with Ronnie is that he thinks everyone is as nice as he is. He's never thought to protect his back in the usual way – by promoting incompetents through his office. He's blown it this time.' And Atkins appeared to have done just that by taking David Marsh, five seats nearer the PM at this dinner, on to his staff. By appearing not to realize what was happening. By apparently assuming gratefully that Marsh was taking all the press briefings out of a concern for his superior's health. Even when the Chief Whip had ventured a quiet word to Ronnie in the Commons Bar about Marsh's frequent pictures in the press, Ronald had merely observed mildly that David Marsh probably helped sell newspapers to young and not-so-young women, and talked affably of other things. Tonight, sipping a cocktail before dinner as he talked to Joseph, he gestured with a movement of his head towards where David Marsh and his wife stood, in front of the press photographers, by the PM, and said, without rancour, 'I suppose everyone thinks I'm a fool. The thing is . . . he wants it all much more than I ever did.'

It was one of those dinner parties which seemed to have little focus beyond a general propaganda about how well the government was doing in catering for the health service, the inner cities, education, housing, old people. It was sprinkled with television celebrities, urbanely preening themselves in the camera flashes, sneaking into corner frame wherever possible. Early in the evening it had seemed that the reason for the party might be civil rights. A dissident Soviet psychiatrist, recently disbursed from the Gulag under pressure from the West, was invited to the podium.

He was small, balding, and might have been stocky in the days before the Gulag had pared his neck to stringy sinews and had stooped his back. He spoke with an intense passion, apparently oblivious to the cocktail-party chatter which had modulated, in lip service to good manners, into a lower register. He derided *glasnost* as merely an image without substance which the West had found it expedient to accept rather than face the truth. There were, he said, other words being used by the General Secretary in preparation for their export to the

West: *uskorenie* – meaning acceleration: *perestroika* – meaning restructuring. England's great poet, Geoffrey Chaucer, had talked of the smiler with the knife under his cloak. But the West had been seduced by images and catch-phrases. In the past they had held up the spectre of Communism, of Reds under the bed. Now they would collude in suggesting that East and West had reached significant agreement on arms reduction. But nothing would have changed. Everything was as it had always been. Cosmetics could only improve an ugly face – not change it.

The Foreign Secretary stepped forward and asked for applause. His tone held the mildest note of reproof, the slightest hint that, though the speech had been very interesting and all that, what would a disaffected Soviet psychiatrist know about the realities and compromises of East–West politics? There was a desultory burst of clapping.

During the dinner Atkins had said, just after talking about David Marsh, 'I couldn't take the other dirty things we do. Under the sheets, I mean. Away from the public gaze.' When Joseph said awkwardly, 'It isn't always possible to reach commendable ends without soiling your hands,' Atkins said, 'Do you remember the furore when Powell made his rivers of blood speech? The refusal to listen? The liberal outcry? That's what really happened here tonight, except that nobody thinks it even worth commenting on Sherdlov.'

The lights and noise bothered Joseph. After dinner he sat with a drink on one of the red plush seats facing an open french window. The pain had begun to needle behind his breastbone again, and he took a couple of indigestion tablets. Ronald Atkins's disaffection had crystallized some sense of unease in him. Perhaps, he reflected, his own comments to Andre sprang from some deeper well in himself than he had known. He found himself thinking of a City dealer he had defended on a charge of insider dealing. Guilty, guilty, guilty, he had known from the moment he had shaken the plump white hand with the gold Rolex on the wrist. One of the many times over the past forty years when his moral nature rose in outrage against the tenets of his professional training. It was not only the death of religion, the post-Freudian substitution of a range of liberal understandings against the old idea of sin, the consumerist propaganda which daily, insidiously, everywhere suggested that material benefits were the *summum vitae*. With a sense almost of shock he recalled his father talking of the English as the Gadarene swine, almost fifty years before. He laughed to himself gently, thinking, perhaps this is what happens when you grow old, when you forget the pleasures of ownership.

A very pretty woman walked through the crowd of people standing under the chandeliers and sat down by him. Her hand was dry and cool, and her smile suggested that she did not, could not, see him as an obese, ugly old man. 'I'm Lydia Marsh,' she said. 'I've always wanted to meet you' – making it sound true, something she had often thought about. He said, 'I gather your husband is to be congratulated,' lost for a moment for the right words to say, diffident about the compliment, a little awkward away from his common ground. He was immediately aware that everything was not entirely well, just by watching her eyes slide away from his for a moment to look down at her hands, now fists, lying in her lap. 'I suppose so,' she said, looking at him, and he could feel, behind her eyes which now regarded him so seriously, some hint that there was more to say if only she could bring herself to start.

But she only stood and held out her hand, saying with odd, stilted formality, 'It was nice to meet you,' and Joseph saw David Marsh making his way through the crowd towards them, the professional smile neatly in place on his regular, tanned features. Marsh glanced briefly at Joseph, the smile a fraction wider for an instant, then guided Lydia by the arm into the crowd again, talking into her ear as they walked.

The party had thinned. Joseph glanced at his watch. Another twenty minutes before Hastings was due with the car. He saw George Maskelyne, wearily elegant, listening (George rarely talked himself if he could avoid it) to Ronald Atkins, one arm folded across his waist, the long fingers of his other hand rubbing gently at his cheek. He glanced at Joseph and nodded, saying something to Atkins before beginning to make his way over. Over forty years, Joseph thought, watching the tall figure walking towards him. And I knew as much about George after the first ten days as I know now. When they were young officers together Joseph had felt hurt by George's aloofness, his apparent indifference to warmth or censure. Then, with the self-absorption of youth, he had seen George's indifference as something personal. Now he knew that George was the same with everyone: there was no grace or favour or sentiment, only deep revolving George himself, playing his games of patriotism and honour, looking (and here Joseph confessed a moment's wry envy) no more than fifty. It was at Julia's funeral that Joseph had finally seen George as he was. George had shed no tears for his wife, had walked erect, in black, over the springy turf, ignoring the rain. Had only said to Joseph, walking by his side, bereft of words of comfort, 'Yes. It was unexpected. Death always is. But there is nothing for it but to cancel and pass on . . . ' There was a Senecan side to George.

Now he sat by Joseph, crossing his legs, resting the glass of brandy on his knee. David and Lydia Marsh stood on the other side of the room, talking to Anton Sherdlov. The psychiatrist was talking animatedly, gesturing energetically with both hands. Marsh nodded from time to time, the professional smile still in place, his eyes constantly ranging across towards the remaining guests. Maskelyne flicked a smudge of ash meticulously from his knee and said drily, 'One of the new men, our Mr Marsh. Got the distinct impression that I wasn't important enough for his smile to turn to full beam.' You're piqued, George, Joseph thought, but there was only the usual well-bred, bored indifference on George's face.

George drained his glass and set it down carefully on the floor. 'Sign of the times that a Soviet dissident tells us the truth – and nobody listens.' The echo of Atkins's words came back to Joseph, making him momentarily uneasy. But George had stood up now, smiling, and seemed at ease again. 'We haven't played bridge for a long time. Let's fix an evening soon.'

Outside it had begun to rain. A waiter nodded his apologies to Joseph, moving the chair next to him so that he could reach the french windows and draw them shut. It was time to go home.

'The next party is for Senator Reinecke on Tuesday,' Hastings said, moving slowly across two lanes to turn right into Lower Regent Street.

'Thank you for reminding me, Edward,' Joseph said with mild sarcasm. 'You know how much I enjoy these evenings . . . ' A few years ago he had really looked forward to these parties and dinners. Looking out the window at the rain-darkened pavements of Regent Street, he wondered briefly if he could get Mrs Plunkett to phone through with his regrets. No, he couldn't do it. He sighed regretfully. Senator Reinecke was notoriously thin-skinned. Besides, much as he disliked to acknowledge it, the social engagements, the image-making went in parallel with his directorships, his charitable works; they were part of the deal.

He fell asleep easily, as always. But his last thought, slipping over the edge into the dark landscape where the strange and distorted tales of night unfolded, was of George's face, briefly revealed, human for a moment.

It was three by the luminous dial of his bedside clock when he awoke, though this, too, had become such a habit that he had no need to look at the time. Lying in the dark, he remembered an English lesson, almost sixty years before.

Mr Watts had sparse red hair, a thin-lipped, humorous mouth, a tendency to dart to the blackboard and draw strange diagrams to illustrate his point. They *almost*, though not quite, meant something, like a shape tantalizingly always just out of sight. And Watts knew. He would fold his arms and sit on his desk with a leg swinging, looking from one face to another with that good-natured smile, and would say, 'I want you to tell me. I want you to do the work.' It was always exciting. Sometimes there would be a curl of smoke from the pocket in which he would put his pipe as they filed in and somebody would put his hand up, leaping up and down with the excitement, saying, 'Sir, sir, sir,' and pointing, until Watts would say something like, 'Just wanted to test that you were awake,' throwing his jacket on the floor and stamping until the smoke cleared and there was the rank after-smell of charred tobacco in the room. Volto Watts, they called him, dead these many years under the sod in his beloved Malvern.

It was that day that Watts, walking through the door and slinging his jacket carelessly across the desk, had turned and pointed, saying, 'What is a symbol, Perkins?' and Perkins had said, with immense seriousness, 'Two round plates of metal with a hand grip behind each which you bash together at . . . ' he looked at the ceiling, making tumpty-tumpty-tum gestures with his hands, 'you know, sir, with the beat.'

The beat currently being a euphemism for an erection there was considerable laughter. Watts smiled, waiting for the sound to die away, and said, 'Excellent. A practical example of a symbol. The word "beat" to your perverse little minds stands for something entirely different. Which means, whenever it is mentioned, you *cognoscenti* derive a secondary and totally separate set of associations . . . '

It was me, Joseph thought, that he asked to read Blake's

poem, remembering how at first the mystery had been there in the words, but too far, too dim, too irrevelant to hold his attention. But suddenly, when Watts had begun to talk, it was as though a window had opened somewhere inside, through which the light, so bright it almost hurt, had flooded ever since. It could not be shut, because once he had seen it, felt it for himself, it worked for so many things. Volto had told them, now all listening, no fidgeting, how at one level the poem was about a rose which was being destroyed by a worm; of how Blake, visionary and moralist, was also at the same time using a metaphor in which the worm was a man's penis (no giggling), and the rose the woman's sexual organ, and 'the howling storm' the storm of sexual passion which Blake and his contemporaries feared and warned against. Of how, again, the rose was England, and the invisible worm was civil unrest, the private vices, sloth, indolence, hatred.

That day (and Joseph could remember the sun slanting against the window, Pearson's face in his hands as he watched Volto, the strange hieroglyphics on the blackboard) Joseph felt, for the first time, the denseness and complexity of life: how things were not necessarily what they seemed, how people spoke one thing but meant another, how the depths went on and on, changing, transmuting, how life was not controllable, but to be experienced with faith, with belief, for that was the only way.

When he had remembered it all, he slept again, not waking until Mrs Denton brought his morning tea.

PART ONE

1

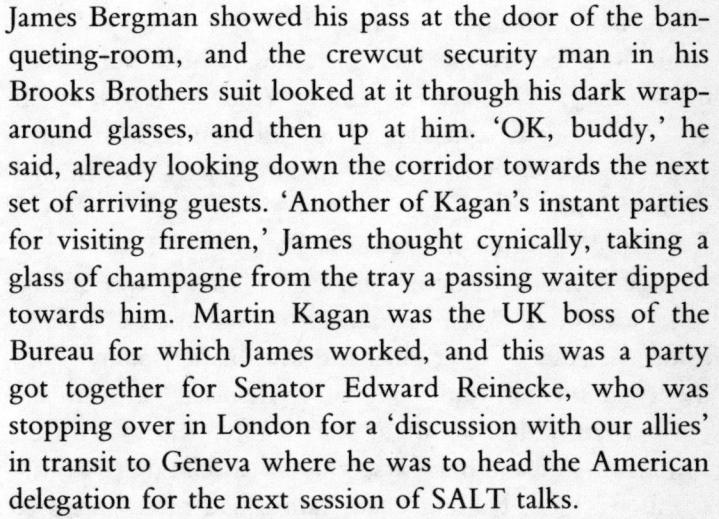

James Bergman showed his pass at the door of the banqueting-room, and the crewcut security man in his Brooks Brothers suit looked at it through his dark wraparound glasses, and then up at him. 'OK, buddy,' he said, already looking down the corridor towards the next set of arriving guests. 'Another of Kagan's instant parties for visiting firemen,' James thought cynically, taking a glass of champagne from the tray a passing waiter dipped towards him. Martin Kagan was the UK boss of the Bureau for which James worked, and this was a party got together for Senator Edward Reinecke, who was stopping over in London for a 'discussion with our allies' in transit to Geneva where he was to head the American delegation for the next session of SALT talks.

Since his wife, poised, sophisticated, had left him James always felt slightly insecure, unsure of himself at functions such as these. He had dreaded this evening for weeks, since his father-in-law, Brigadier Maskelyne, had given him the invitation with the wry, knowing smile of a man who is half amused to be the bearer of bad tidings. There was no question of refusing, of course. It was as good as an order from the Bureau. But he felt he had only been asked to make up the numbers.

He stood at the edge of the hall, by a loaded buffet table

covered in white linen, and outside caterers' delicacies, watching the guests. Women had usually found him attractive, in large part because he seemed totally unaware of their admiration. He still weighed the same as he had when he was playing football at Harvard as a twenty-year-old, fifteen years before, and he moved with the natural grace of a man who kept his body in condition. Something indefinable about him, the wariness of the blue eyes, the slight tightness of his mouth, suggested a secretive nature. But he gave the impression of a man who possessed the ability to think, and reason, and act upon his conclusions. In those first few weeks of marriage, long before the final bitterness which had seeped everywhere, destroyed everything, Anna used to hold his arm possessively and say, 'They all wanted you, but I won . . . ' But she had tired of all her trophies finally, even of him.

He looked round the room at the guests. They were a strange mixture. Senator Reinecke, the host, was talking to James's boss, Kagan, emphasizing some point by slamming the edge of his right hand into his left palm. They made an incongruous contrast – Reinecke as lean and tense as an athlete about to start a race, Kagan with his shirt crumpled and his sparse ginger hair clinging sweatily to his freckled, balding head. James had often surmised that Kagan had got to run the London office of the Bureau precisely because nobody could ever see him as a threat. But there was now, as always, a hint of insolence in his apparently obsequious manner. He was a man with a long memory and few friends. Like Hoover he believed that knowledge is strength, and if his rise had not been meteoric, he had survived a number of departmental fiascos which had seen bigger men fall. For some unfathomable reason he liked James, a fact observed by James's contemporaries with the Bureau, Carter and

Rivers. It had set him apart, like a schoolboy who is singled out for praise by a master. Just wait until we get you in the playground, their glances seemed to say. But now we're all grown up it won't go further, James reasoned, whenever the insight struck him afresh.

James finished his drink and took another. Better be careful, he thought. He'd have to keep his wits about him tonight. Even if he didn't shine on social occasions, he didn't want black marks on his career sheet. In the far corner he saw George Maskelyne talking to a young MP. It took a moment before he could remember the name. David Marsh, the power behind the MoD, due to take over at any time now. A really high flier. Marsh's wife, Lydia, stood by his side, watching her husband. James felt a strange sense of loss, remembering Anna looking at him like that. Behind him a woman's voice said mockingly, 'Making up the numbers, James?' and he turned to find Sally Kane.

Maskelyne must have brought her. She, in turn, had probably provided at least half the young ladies wandering round the party with such elegant sophistication, as though Embassy parties were their daily entertainment. He felt suddenly at ease. 'Hello, Sally,' he said with genuine warmth, and she laughed at the apparent surprise in his voice. Even knowing what she did for a living he felt a momentary stirring of desire, looking down at the full laughing mouth, the curve of her breasts under the thin, cream silk dress.

'Most of them are whores, dear,' she said, putting on a mock East End accent. 'One of your boss's instant parties for the Senator.' She took his arm and led him over to a corner away from the press of people. He could feel the heat of her body against his side. He had the uncomfortable feeling that she was laughing at him. It was the same feeling he had often experienced in his father-in-law's company. That they both found him amusing, but would never let him into the secret.

'Tell me some names,' he said, not really interested, but to keep her with him, and she gave him a look of mock surprise.

'The big, ugly man talking to Senator Reinecke. That's Sir Joseph Sainsbury, the lawyer the press refer to as the cleverest man in England. He served with the Brigadier during the last war. The man over there with his wife . . . ' she gestured with her glass towards David Marsh, spilling a few drops of champagne down her dress, 'is Mr Marsh . . . ' There was a trace of mockery, a momentary lewd inflection in her voice, and he turned to look at her. She feigned innocence. 'Oh . . . and there . . . ' gesturing towards a large, florid man with Edwardian mutton-chop side-whiskers, 'is Professor Butterfield. He's something to do with the research establishment at Porton Down.'

She went on thus for a moment. About one or two of the men she ventured a salacious comment. 'Married with two children, but gay as all get out, my dear. Found in his garage tied to a ladder, flogged senseless, a couple of years ago. His lawyer kept it out of the papers . . . ' Of an instantly recognizable aristocrat she whispered behind her hand, 'He was the headless waiter in that big scandal in the sixties.' But it was the tolerant malice of the mature woman, and James found, as always, that a few moments in her company made him sad that she had chosen to become a whore. Once he had asked her why. 'Money and power, dear,' she had answered, her tone more clipped than usual.

At seven forty-five Edward Reinecke took the microphone at the end of the long room, and held up his hand for silence. The buzz of conversation died away. As Reinecke began to speak Sally dug Bergman in the ribs, and he stifled an insane desire to giggle, imagining the gravitas of tomorrow's newspaper reports. How many of the readers would have the faintest idea that the glittering company surrounding the Senator with such apparent rapt attention were good-time girls?

Reinecke was impressive, nevertheless. There was a demagoguery there which overcame the clichés, and stirred Bergman's patriotism. The words rose above the whispered conversations, the clink of glasses, and reminded James of the oath he had sworn when he first joined the Bureau.

'My friends, lords, ladies and gentlemen. In a few weeks' time I shall be in Geneva with my team to embark on a new round of SALT talks with the Russians. I believe that they too have the same hopes in their hearts, the same ideals in their minds. That they too perceive this meeting as possibly the most important attempt in the history of mankind to prevent a catastrophe of unimaginable dimensions. I have no doubt there will be rhetoric on both sides: there will be accusations of bad faith; reminders of each other's conduct in lesser matters over the years; there will be tough talking and bitter words, too. But I have no doubt that the Soviet Union has the same perceptions as we Americans, we Europeans, we citizens of the free world. That, though we cannot set the clock back and destroy the knowledge we have created, we can now see that it is a monster which requires our deepest thoughts, our strongest faith, our most profound recognition of our common humanity – and the threat to it – to overcome. I ask you to pledge your prayers and best wishes to success – not for us alone, but for all mankind.'

There was a burst of cheering and Reinecke was instantly surrounded as he stepped off the podium. James shivered. Between the action and the response, falls the shadow.

He felt Sally stir at his side. 'You wouldn't like to come home with me tonight?' she asked, and Bergman felt again the instinctive puritanism which denied him what his body craved.

'Oh well,' she said. 'Perhaps I'll take the Senator when he's finished with his admirers.'

Getting his coat from the cloakroom, Bergman wondered if she really meant it. Despite his years in England he had never learnt when the English were being serious and when they were only joking.

Outside the windows of the club, perched on the corner of St James's and Piccadilly, the rain beat down on the drenched pavements from a blue-black sky, though the buildings were lit with the last pastel rays of the sun. The club was agreeably old-fashioned, its membership in the main composed of elderly gentlemen who greeted each other warmly, had watery vacant blue eyes, pink skins and tobacco-stained moustaches, and who reminisced with each other about one of the Great Wars, or about Suez or the Profumo affair. There was a certain comfortable somnolence, a sense that all great things had long passed from the earth, that the membership was now settling down, fairly happily on the whole, to get on with the business of living out the littleness of the remainder of their lives.

Joseph Sainsbury had first introduced Maskelyne to the club shortly after the war and occasionally, when their respective duties permitted, one or other would make up a bridge four at the other's invitation. 'The dinosaurs' graveyard,' Joseph used to say. 'I only got in because three of them couldn't distinguish between a black and a white ball.' But in addition to its gentle vices of snobbishness and exclusivity, it did have virtues. It had saved many a marriage, affording congenial and sympathetic company, and a bed after the clarets and brandies, to members temporarily sheltering from conjugal storms. And it afforded a genuine dependability, a resistance to change. The worn brown leather furniture, the gold-embossed, unread books standing in ancient glass-fronted mahogany cabinets. The attendants, none below sixty, who servilely shuffled over the faded Wilton carpets about their business, dressed in the shiny black waistcoats and striped trousers of a bygone age. Many of the members had never been abroad, despite their far-flung business interests. There was a patriotism of a curious brand abroad here in many of the members, a distillation of Sir Henry Newbolt, Kipling, and Churchill's war-time speeches.

James Bergman hated the club, which was probably why his father-in-law invited him there for their infrequent meetings. There was in Maskelyne some hint of the beliefs of a former age: that suffering formed the character and bitter medicine did the most good. Walking in the heavy drizzle under his umbrella, James had wished again, as he had so often over the past few days, that this operation was entirely American. At least he knew where he stood with Kagan: there would have been none of this subtle, eyebrow-raising stuff the British went in for – just a profanely delivered set of instructions to do the job in the most efficient way. He looked warily at the doorman on the way in, half convinced by the man's suave manner that he too possessed some secret, innate superiority. 'Probably read history at Cambridge,' he reflected to himself sourly, walking across the carpet to where Maskelyne sat reading the *Financial Times*, with a whisky on the table by his chair.

He put his folder on the table and sat down, picking up the drink Maskelyne had ordered in anticipation of his arrival. Maskelyne put down his paper, glancing briefly at James over the gold-rimmed half glasses he affected, and picked up the folder. He looked round, as though to satisfy himself that there was no one close enough to peer over his shoulder. A few old gentlemen sat around a table at the far end, their murmurations dimly audible across the wide floor. The barman polished the glasses and held them up to the light for inspection. Maskelyne opened the folder and took out the photographs with his long, thin fingers, studying them one by one. They were grainy and indistinct, like *paparazzi*'s photographs of royalty taking a dip on holiday. Maskelyne made a clicking sound with his tongue which could have indicated disapproval, and began to look through them again under the lamp by his side.

James watched his father-in-law from his deep leather chair on the other side of the occasional table, hoping to pick up some hint of approval. Wryly he wondered at himself: in the six years he had known the Brigadier he had never seen the mask of indifferent world-weariness drop: not at his daughter's wedding, or in the cold light of dawn at the spy exchange by the Wall in '83. Not even, he remembered, by Julia's graveside that cold September morning, five years ago. He'd quoted Bishop King's Exequy then: 'But hark, my pulse, like a soft Drum, Beats my approach, tells Thee I come, And slow howe'er my Marches be, I shall at last lie down by Thee', and it had seemed strange, out of character. But the coldness was there, even then. And, like Joseph, James had seen that Maskelyne's detachment was from everyone, from everything. It had been unrealistic for him to expect to break through that reserve merely because he had married the Brigadier's daughter: the thaw he had expected when they first married had never come. Now, of course, Anna was a subject they never discussed. And, without evidence, James nevertheless felt that the Brigadier's wintry manner hid some disapproval of him for not playing the man properly, for not keeping his wife in check.

He caught the eye of a passing waiter and signalled for their glasses to be refilled. Maskelyne looked up over his half glasses.

'It's undoubtedly Alexandrevitch. But what does that prove?'

Bergman took the photographs and put them back into the folder. He couldn't suppress a momentary feeling of bitterness, a sense he had so often experienced that Maskelyne wished to diminish him, not for any personal reason, but because he represented the hated Americans. For what had become evident to him, in the off-duty hours he had spent with the Brigadier, was the chauvinistic flavour of Maskelyne's Powellite Toryism. He hated the American presence in Britain, he hated the Common Market, he hated the rights of appeal to the International Court at Strasbourg, because these were all to him the concrete evidence of Britain's decline and the End of Empire. Now, with the presence of Cruise missiles on British soil, and with the seeming importance of the coming Strategic Arms Limitation Talks which Reinecke was conducting on behalf of the senior partner in the Western Alliance, there had been a perceptible shift in London towards the Americans taking the lead in certain matters. Though he knew it was nothing personal, the insight made it no easier to stomach Maskelyne's barbed shafts. Typically perverse of Kagan to give him this end of a shitty stick, James thought ruefully. Why the hell he hadn't chosen Carter or Rivers was beyond comprehension.

He leaned across the table and lowered his voice. Not that there was likely to be any subversive elements in the noisy group who had just walked by – particularly in a club whose membership was largely comprised of aristocratic English landowners in their upper seventies. Still, there had been Blunt, and you never knew.

'You know as well as I do, sir, that only the trusted few share the podium with the General Secretary on these occasions. We've had expert analysis. The photograph is genuine.'

Maskelyne sat back in his chair so that his thin, sardonic face was in shadow. For want of something to do, James took out the photographs and looked at them again. It was the May Day Parade. The first picture, taken with a long-focus lens, showed the missiles in Red Square, with the balcony marked out to demonstrate the parameters of the blow-up. In the succeeding photographs the huge picture of Lenin appeared clearly, with a mass of figures in Russian hats on the balcony. In the foreground Gorbachev, Gromyko and other dignitaries of the CCCP. And behind them, goddammit, Alexandrevitch. It had taken Kagan's boys, anticipating the problem of identification, two weeks to come up with a colour coding which would give positive identification under certain chemical applications in the darkroom. The suit material wasn't patented, but it was unlikely that anyone else working in this part of the periphery of the business would be concerned to produce a material with certain chromatic features for photographic identification. Everything checked out. It *was* Alexandrevitch.

Maskelyne cleared his throat irritably. He folded the gold-rimmed glasses with his neat, precise gestures, and slid them into a leather case. He leaned back in his chair again so that the other man could barely distinguish his features in the gloom, and said in his dry, pedantic voice (the one he uses to lecture us, Bergman thought), 'Let's take the CIA assumptions as read for the moment . . . ' He placed the fingers of both hands together, resting his elbows on the leather arms of the chair. His voice held the merest cadence of disbelief.

'We've had to accept your assurances that he has truly turned. Yes, I know about the wife and daughter under surveillance in Oregon,' he waved Bergman's attempt at interruption away, 'but you are dealing with ideologues here. Remember the man who put his pregnant girlfriend on a flight with a bomb in her luggage? It may well be that Alexandrevitch is no different. But let's surmise that he really has come over. How will he get the story over in Moscow?'

Bergman paused while the waiter put down their drinks on the monogrammed doilies. From the far corner an elderly gentleman spluttered with laughter at something his companion had said. Outside the window lightning flared briefly, and thunder rumbled distantly in the west.

He was glad of a moment's respite. This was the question he had been dreading, and Kagan had been of little help in the briefing session. He'd only made the usual comment about being unable to make an omelette without breaking eggs. 'Come on, Jimmy. I can't do everything for you. The guy's your father-in-law. That must count for something. Besides, that's the game plan we all agreed. We can't change now.' And Kagan had given the impression of some irrevocable decision taken by men who couldn't be troubled again with such trivia.

James moved to the edge of his chair so that he could see Maskelyne's face. He said carefully, 'Our strategists say that to make this one stick there will have to be a sacrifice. No pawns this time, but a bishop at least. Nothing less will convince Kalevsky.' In the pause that followed he wondered if he'd overplayed his hand with the words 'our strategists'. That had been Kagan and Rivers in shirtsleeves with a pack of Budweisers ruminating on the situation while watching the football.

Maskelyne stood up abruptly. His grey suit was immaculate, and he stood like an officer on drill parade. 'Let's walk a moment. It's getting stuffy in here.'

They crossed the road and walked past the Ritz in silence. The rain had almost died away now, and there was a freshness in the air. Walking behind Maskelyne, James felt a familiar sense of rising anger. He could never find a way to overcome the sense of inferiority he always felt in the other man's presence. Even in those early days of his marriage when he and Anna had stayed with Julia and Maskelyne, and Maskelyne had showed a rather touching enthusiasm for the plants in his spacious garden, the air of effortless superiority prevailed. 'You see this lithospermum over here. As a member of the RHS I was able to obtain a special licence to import it. Unusual to see it doing so well under these conditions . . . ' The trick, if trick there were, was his ability always to take the lead, to lay down the ground rules, to control the direction of the conversation.

The sodium lamps cast a yellow glow on the grass in St James's Square. There were a few people walking down the diagonal path linking Piccadilly with Victoria. On one of the still-damp benches a couple were kissing passionately, and Bergman, half ashamed of his prurient curiosity, watched the boy's hand move up the girl's thigh. 'People are watching,' she said in a reproving tone, and the boy laughed dismissively, moving closer.

Maskelyne sat at the end of an empty bench. Overhead the sound of a jet came faintly over the traffic noise. James sat down, folding his hands together on his lap like a schoolboy about to be reprimanded.

'You Americans . . . ' Maskelyne said, and it was hard to judge whether contempt or amusement lay behind the words. 'Everything is acceptable to you in the interests of expediency. I understand the mechanism you wish to operate, but I deplore the morality behind it.' He fell silent until a couple had passed the bench, and had walked on out of earshot. 'To use your jargon, I know who's expendable at the moment. And I know how it can be done. You'll have to give me the timing, of course.'

Bergman said defensively, 'I'm only following orders, sir . . . ' and Maskelyne smiled briefly, getting to his feet and brushing an imaginary speck of dust from his raincoat. 'I remember Nuremberg,' he said. 'That's what they all said.'

2

At forty-one David Marsh seemed to be on the brink of fulfilling his early promise. He had been born the second son of a wealthy landowning aristocrat, and had learned early that there was no virtue in coming second. His elder brother, one of those men who are settled into comfortable middle age by thirty, had inherited the title, the 22,000 acres of prime farmland, and the bulk of the investment income. David, from an early age only able to look enviously at those who had progressed beyond him, had to grit his teeth and be content with an Eton education, a first in PPE at Balliol and the presidency of the Union. With an income from a trust fund which sufficed to take care of the necessities of life he had gone on from Oxford to come third in the Civil Service examinations, followed by a tour as Second Assistant in Saigon, followed by a tour as First Secretary in Washington. When he decided it was time to move on from the Civil Service and enter politics, it was a foregone conclusion that the Tories would offer him a safe seat in one of their shire strongholds, and just as certain that he would rise rapidly to ministerial rank. He had the attributes of a forties matinée idol – a permanent suntan, regular, handsome features and a brilliant smile. Inevitably he had a number of detractors, particularly among Ronnie Atkins' circle of friends. The jury was about equally divided between warm approval and finger-wagging jealousy. 'Too clever by half' was a phrase much heard among his critics, though another, 'too good to be true', contained more truth.

For there was a fatal flaw which not even his unkindest critic had suspected, and which his adoring and beautiful wife, Lydia, was trying to ignore, despite the telltale signs. It was almost, indeed, something which David himself, for all his apparent brilliance, did not recognize in himself, being a man totally without any faculty for introspection. He saw himself as the media portrayed him, and loved himself as they appeared to love him. He saw a man who had succeeded, who had married a beautiful wife, had provided his two sons with the best education money could buy.

But Sally Kane, whom David visited from time to time in her flat near Shepherd's Market, saw with the eyes of experience what David himself could never see. When George Browning, an old Oxford friend (unknown to David, a toiler in George Maskelyne's vineyard), had first taken David to meet her after a few drinks on the terrace at the House, she had assessed him with cruel accuracy: the product of a puritan upbringing and a public school education, whose early idealization of his wife had in some measure returned; who in part had become bored by her, and in part could no longer bear the guilt of defiling her with his perverse and gross lusts: a man, in short, who had been reared on the doctrine that women could only at best endure men's sexuality. So that, when the burning fires which had overcome these feelings in the early days had died down, he now shrank from approaching her. It was a maiming Sally had seen all too often in her 'practice' (as she liked to think of it), where Cabinet Ministers rubbed shoulders with eminent lawyers, and super salesmen drank in the seductive bar with prominent churchmen. She was wont to reflect that it was the public school system, more than any other factor, which had brought her wealth and cynicism in roughly equal measure, but she had retained enough humanity occasionally to feel sad at such waste.

Largely because there was so little routine in their marriage, it had taken some time for Lydia to admit the changes to herself. At first their infrequent love-making had begun to take on a perfunctory, almost abstracted aspect. Then he had suggested that they sleep in separate bedrooms because his duties often kept him late at the House and he didn't want to disturb her. He had ignored the unspoken question in her face, kissing her lightly after he told her. 'Won't change anything really,' he said, laughing and ruffling her hair. 'Anyway, it's a slightly undignified procedure at our age.' She had managed to smile as though it were all right, almost determined, now, not to show him how the words had hurt her. But soon, between dealing with the boys and organizing their own increasingly busy social life, the pain had muted. 'He will come back in time,' she told herself. 'It happens to many men in middle life.' Somewhere, too, sitting on committees with other political wives of an age or a few years older, she began to feel no longer apart, but included in a sisterhood of common, though largely unvoiced, experience. It was a small comfort, but better than nothing.

Two days after Maskelyne and Bergman had met at the club there was a ring on the doorbell of the Marshes' Buckinghamshire home. Lydia had been taking advantage of the rainy morning to reorganize David's study, and when she came down the stairs their housekeeper, Mrs Baines, was ushering two men into the hall. 'These gentlemen want to make an appointment to see Mr Marsh,' she said, and Lydia smiled mechanically, indicating the sitting-room. 'It's all right, Mrs Baines. Perhaps you could bring us some coffee and biscuits.' She felt an instant, unplaceable sense of unease.

The older of the two had a spurious, white-haired respectability which sat easily with his well-cut suit. But his heavy features, prognathous jaw and heavy-lidded eyes hinted at a blunt, disturbing brutality. There seemed, too, some menace in his manner, though he shook hands and smiled pleasantly enough in introducing himself. 'I'm James Avery . . . and this is Roger Burberry. We've just come to ask a few questions about your husband. Just routine, you understand.' The understated words, the very normality of the sun struggling through the clouds on to the grass outside the french windows, the coffee tray laid with three cups – all seemed slightly unreal to Lydia for a moment. Avery sat easily on the sofa, and she noted abstractedly that his shoes had seen better days.

'What questions?' Lydia asked, wondering if she should ask for any form of identification. As though he had read her thoughts, Avery reached into his breast pocket and held out a plastic card-holder for a moment before putting it away, gazing at her intently all the while. There was something disconcerting about the directness of his gaze, the wetness of the too-full lips. 'Security. We carry out what is called positive vetting from time to time. It's standard procedure. Nothing to worry about.' The professional manner stayed impeccably in place. Beside him on the sofa Burberry shifted slightly and examined his nails. Lydia felt cold. There was something disconcerting in the way Avery kept trying to reassure her which had the opposite effect.

Avery took a photograph from his wallet and passed it to Lydia. His hands had a puffy, dead whiteness. 'I must ask if you know this woman, Mrs Marsh.' Looking at the picture she felt again the sense of unease. It was a blurred colour slide of a girl in a low-cut, vee-necked white sweater, holding a glass and smiling at something beyond the frame of the picture. The face had a hard prettiness, and Lydia found it disquietingly familiar, just out of reach. She said, hesitantly, 'I don't think I've met her. But her face seems familiar . . . ' The two men exchanged a brief glance.

Mrs Baines came in to clear away the tray. Seddon, the gardener, toiled past the window, pushing a barrowload of manure. At the edge of the lawn a robin tugged fiercely at a worm for a second and then flew away. Lydia felt a sense of panic: What's happening, she thought. Why are these men showing me this picture? What have they to do with us? And beneath, fears and suspicions began to grow, not yet fully articulated but already seeming to fit into some half-perceived pattern.

Avery took the photograph from her. When Mrs Baines had gone, with slow, reluctant steps, he said easily, 'You'll have seen her picture in the papers, I expect. She runs a high-class vice ring. Mainly visiting dignitaries, Embassy staff, prominent businessmen and their friends. She had a short spell in prison some time ago . . . ' He smiled without humour.

Suddenly, violently almost, Lydia said, 'I don't see what any of this has to do with David.'

Burberry said soothingly, 'We're not suggesting it does, Mrs Marsh.' He had spaniel's eyes, soft and confiding.

Avery stood up. He moved like a boxer, swaying slightly on the balls of his feet. 'One last question, Mrs Marsh. Do you know the Soviet attaché, Mr Pyotr Alexandrevitch?'

Lydia remembered a small man, permanently smiling, invariably dressed in a badly-cut blue double-breasted suit. Very jolly, with an oddly endearing habit of misusing English colloquialisms. It had been something of a mystery to see him amongst the businessmen and politicians who came to their parties, but David had said, 'He makes me laugh. You need a few people like that in this job,' and she had grown quite fond of the little Russian in the end. Then she had liked anyone who made David feel good.

'Yes,' she said. 'He used to come here to our parties from time to time. I don't know anything about him, I'm afraid . . . '

Avery seemed satisfied. He followed Burberry to the front door. Almost as an afterthought, he turned and said, 'We'll need to see your husband, of course. Perhaps you'll let him know we'll be calling to arrange a meeting.'

When they walked down the steps out into the weak sunlight, Mrs Baines came out of the kitchen. They both watched the anonymous black Ford begin to move down the gravelled drive through the side window. 'Is everything all right, ma'am?' she asked anxiously, her hands folded over her apron.

Lydia forced brightness into her smile. 'Of course, Mrs Baines. What could possibly be wrong? They're just carrying out routine checks, that's all.'

But she found it difficult to concentrate for the rest of the day. The thoughts she tried to push away kept intruding, so that she would start a job and then forget what she was doing. She wondered about the girl particularly. No matter how hard she tried to dismiss the thoughts, it wasn't possible.

It was dinner with Atkins. David had made a moue, shrugging his shoulders when he told her, as though to indicate that he was sorry, but there it was. Surprised, she had said, 'But I like Ronald and Elizabeth. He's been very good to you, hasn't he?' and had felt uneasy, almost angry, when he looked at her, his jaw truculently set, and said, 'He didn't give me what I have, you know. I took it.' She'd half known that this side of David existed, but he had hidden enough from her to allow her to dissemble, to say, in the past, that it hadn't existed. It hurt her now that he no longer seemed.to care enough to make the effort.

He'd said little when she'd told him about Avery's visit,

when they were walking round the garden together with a drink before leaving for their dinner engagement. 'Positive vetting. It's normal procedure,' he said curtly, and again she felt hurt, distanced from him. The quick, bright smile he gave her in apology, the hand on her arm, had suddenly felt professional. Like the posing with babies, the confected concern with which he listened to the old widow when he was in mid campaign, the meaningless handshakes. Walking by his side she had silently chided herself for her disloyalty, but a little anger began to burn, a slight resentment that he had begun to take her for granted.

When she had mentioned the girl's picture, saying, despite herself, 'Quite pretty in a tarty sort of way,' he had moved his head suddenly away from her. It may have been to follow the sudden flight of a thrush (she told herself, desperately trying to avoid the suspicions which had begun to gnaw), but it felt as though he were hiding his face from her. 'Look. I haven't anything to hide,' he said, his voice edged, rebarbative, and she nodded, thinking desperately, I didn't accuse you of anything: why deny something if it doesn't exist to be denied? As they were walking back from the folly (planned together when they were first married), the neat vistas of flower beds, the artful, stunted willows, the Victorian conservatory, seemed already to have lost some charm, invested in them (for her) by the joint planning which had gone into their making. Talking to friends who suspected their husbands were being unfaithful had, in the past, given her a feeling of slightly smug security. It was only her mother who had once said, 'Take nothing for granted. Power can do strange things to some men.' But that momentary unease had died away, until now. David was becoming a stranger, and a stranger she didn't even like very much.

Was it her imagination that Ronald and Elizabeth were a shade less welcoming, that there were awkward pauses which had never seemed part of their previous relationship, that there was even a hint of unvoiced disapproval in Ronald's manner? Lydia had always felt grateful that neither of them seemed aware of David's envy before, usually expressed (for later amplification) before their car had left the drive and while their host and hostess were still visible through the rear-view mirror of the car, framed in their Queen Anne portico, waving to their departing guests. On the last occasion David, accelerating the car too fast down the gravel drive, had said, 'It seems so unjust that a nonentity like Atkins has so much. Inherited wealth, power, position . . . ' There was a childish, material envy in him which frightened her. The idealism she had admired when they first met seemed to have faded, to have been replaced by a cynical, mercenary ambition.

Driving to the dinner in silence, she had suddenly realized how few of those early friends they still saw. 'Of what use could he be to us?' David had asked in an unguarded moment, when she had suggested inviting an artist friend from their old Chelsea days down to dinner. And then had been instantly contrite, so that she had, with difficulty now, put away her new fears: *How much? Can he fix it? He owes me.* This was the ugly new vocabulary in which the rites of passage were conducted. And that love, once so apparently whole-hearted, passionate, all-embracing, was becoming hedged about by compromise. Other things, too. 'Why don't you wear the Cartier necklace? If you have it, flaunt it,' he had said earlier in the evening. And somewhere she had already begun to mourn his loss.

Over dinner (avocado and crab, sorbet, venison in red wine, *rumptopf* and cream, with appropriate wines), Lydia picked at her food and tried to listen to Elizabeth talking about her charity programmes for bilharzia in Africa, and eye operations in India. Elizabeth's white hands flapped in enthusiasm, and she fixed Lydia with her faded blue eyes with a manic stare, as though daring her to lose attention for even a second. Across the table Lydia heard Ronald lower his voice and say, 'Is the Butterfield scenario still going ahead? and David responding confidently, 'Of course. The PM likes it,' with the aggressive bravado which, even now, spoke to her of the little boy. Elizabeth paused expectantly, and Lydia nodded, hoping the gesture was appropriate. At the other end of the table Ronald was saying doubtfully, 'I feel these things are prone to go wrong. Intelligence has moved forward so much since Powers was shot down, since the Bay of Pigs . . . ' He sounded tired. Across the table Elizabeth leaned forward, her nose a prow of light under the chandelier, saying, 'So I can count on your support?' and Lydia nodded again, wondering what she had committed herself to.

For an hour after dinner it was a little more like old times. Sanderson, the butler, saw to their drinks, and closed the french windows to shut out the rain which had started while they dined. David, at his ingenuous, boyish best, told stories against himself, about Saigon and Washington. Laughing with the others despite herself, Lydia saw that it was just another trick. David had never been so inept. He was merely charming Ronald and Elizabeth. And was succeeding, of course. She felt lonelier than ever.

Whether it would have comforted her to eavesdrop on Ronald and Elizabeth after she and David had left is another matter. She might have felt less alone, but her loyalties would have been strained.

It was a small enough thing. Almost as an afterthought, as they climbed the stairs to the bedroom, Ronald said regretfully, 'That boy has almost everything. Except integrity.' And Elizabeth stopped on the riser above him and put her arms about his neck and kissed him where the hair had receded at the front of his scalp, and said, 'Thank God you're retiring.'

3

George Maskelyne held his glass up to the light, and then sipped his wine appreciatively. To his son-in-law he could invest all his gestures with some sense of tradition, of belonging to an exclusive club whose members alone were the possessors of some arcane knowledge about the right way of doing things. His pleasures, if somebody who showed so little emotion could be said to have pleasures, were all expressed thus: in an inward satisfaction which needed no audience and no sharing of what he had discovered with others. That was not to say he was a sybarite, for, despite the obvious comforts of this house in which the Brigadier's family had lived for six generations, the impression he always gave was that of an ascetic man, to whom the luxuries of the flesh were of little account besides some burning, secret, inner vision.

James Bergman sat at the other end of the polished cherrywood table, nursing his third Jack Daniels. He was not a drinking man, but his visits to his father-in-law were rendered more tolerable by the slight fuzziness a few drinks brought in their wake. They had already talked at some length in the garden, Maskelyne in gardening gauntlets fastidiously pruning the roses and spraying the stems for blackfly, while Bergman walked behind, ill-at-ease in the rural setting. So far, only business, politics, sport. They never talked of Anna, or Julia, or personal things. That was forbidden territory.

Resuming the conversation started in the garden, Bergman said, 'Surely there were others who could have served as well . . . ?', unable to keep the indignation from his voice. Maskelyne looked at him with a cold, impersonal gaze down the long length of the polished table with its centrepiece of Georgian silver on Honiton lace. He said in his precise, clipped tones, 'Our masters dictated what had to be done, but the rest was my choice – had to be. You'll learn in time the value of authenticity. Those old warhorses your people suggested – Horsmann, Dunford, Atkins – they wouldn't do. Kalevsky would see through that immediately. No, it has to be a real, verifiable bishop.'

James said bitterly, 'You've changed your mind since we talked about it in the park. Do you remember your comment about Nuremberg, and your contempt for us? How does all that fit in . . .?'

Maskelyne said with sudden, surprising passion, 'The man's a moral degenerate. That's part of the reason. And, when all's said and done, I'm only a hewer of wood and a drawer of water. Those sentiments I expressed were from the old days when Sir Henry Newbolt's words ruled our lives, and honour and patriotism brought out the best in us. But forty years of peace have taken all that away. We have the Welfare State instead. The right to be paid for doing nothing. The expectation that the State must take care of us . . . '

The subject was closed. At least I've learned to recognize the signals, James thought, his mind idly moving over other things while Maskelyne fell into reminiscence about the war, his companionship with Joseph, the men under his command. This was one familiar trait which was both irritating and humanizing, this habit of slipping into reminiscence after the third glass of port. Not, even now, that

Maskelyne's mask of polite indifference slipped by even a fraction, but his voice changed timbre and seemed to contain some intense, incommunicable excitement stirred by these memories. 'There are no good wars. But it was a time to be young. We had things to do – not all this shuffling of papers and passing of remote judgements in dusty offices. It was a time to be alive . . . '

After dinner they sat in the twilight coming through the french windows. The smell of night-scented stocks hung on the air. Hudson, Maskelyne's factotum, bent, gnarled and silent at seventy, had put Elgar's Enigma Variations on before retiring discreetly. It was always the same: puzzlingly low-brow. But Maskelyne had once said, 'It's the folding and refolding of the themes that touches me. It makes me feel that what I do has a moral purpose.' James had half understood what he meant and, for a time, the comment had made him feel more warmly towards the older man. It held out, tantalizingly beyond reach, the prospect that Maskelyne, too, might be human.

When the music had finished and they were about to retire for the night, Bergman asked curiously, 'I don't suppose you'll tell me what the information we're trying to withhold from Kalevsky is, sir?' and Maskelyne, swaying very slightly, said portentously, touching the side of his nose with his forefinger, 'The secret is the secret, my boy.' He had to be content with that.

4

Anna and Catherine had left Greenham Common two days before. It was Anna who had said, 'Oh, let's just have a couple of days away from it all,' and they had driven down to stay at a pub just outside Salisbury. It's not as though I don't feel committed to the cause, Anna had said to herself, justifying the break. It was just the hopeless stridency, the one-sidedness of what they were doing, which sometimes weighed her down. And, she had to confess to herself, she did miss the attention that men had always given her. It just wasn't enough to see a momentary gleam of attraction in the eye of an advancing policeman. It didn't stop them bundling you into a Black Maria and testifying against you in court; and, besides, nothing could ever come of it.

In fact very little had happened until the day they were due to return. They had done the week's grocery shopping, and the car was already loaded. It was Catherine who got into conversation with the Russian when they had gone into the bar to have a quick drink before setting off. At first Anna stayed out of it, thinking the Russian was trying to pick them up, but he showed none of the moist-eyed prurience she associated with men whose interests were primarily sexual. Soon she found herself talking to him about their campaign, almost apologetically, as though, in his eyes, she and her friend must be identified with the interests of the merchants of death she so despised, whose barbed wire surrounded the compound, whose soldiers stood guard over the obscene weaponry the Americans had foisted upon England.

The Russian had listened for a while, wearing a sceptical smile which began to annoy her. He told them he was taking a couple of weeks' holiday in Wiltshire, and that he worked for Aeroflot in Piccadilly, and she began to feel angry and frustrated that his commitment to the Soviet system seemed to preclude any understanding that they were all essentially on the same side, humanity. 'So you don't approve of what we're doing,' she said aggressively, ready to attack. But he was not at all abashed by the truculence of her tone. Gathering their glasses up clumsily, he said over his shoulder, 'A minute, please,' and made his way over to the bar. When he returned he set them down carefully, smiling at them.

'Don't get me the wrong way. I appreciate your aims, and I clap your attempts to change these policies. But . . . ' with a shrug of his shoulders, ' . . . these demonstrations change nothing. Look at your CND. All that marching and speechmaking for nothing. It only disrupts the traffic.'

Anna sat back in the window-seat with her arms folded, listening. Now she said, 'Well, what do you suggest?', and he pulled his chair forward and leaned his elbows on the table, dropping his voice to a quieter register. 'There are more potent ways. All these Cruise missiles are already accepted. They have already been compensated for on our side. No amount of protesting can change that. But there are things being done here which your public opinion knows nothing about. We have information that a new generation of germ and virus warfare is being tested currently at Porton Down. The delivery method could be via a conventional missile, or through imported foodstuffs, or through our water systems. The viruses are completely resistant to any known antidotes and work through genetic interference with the victim's cell-replicating process. In effect the virus produces a rapidly proliferating carcinogenic reaction in which the visceral cells mutate rapidly – go out of control . . . '

Catherine's white, equine face registered horror. She said disbelievingly, 'But where did you get this information from? It can't be true. They wouldn't allow it.'

A group of men at the bar looked across at the trio curiously. A large, red-faced man, wearing riding boots and a flat cap, sniggered and made an inaudible comment to the rest of the group, and the others laughed loudly and turned back to their beer. Ignorant fools, Anna thought. Her face burned red.

Her husband had been like that. Not quite so obvious; but he hadn't understood, either. Even when she had stood at the door with her case packed, he had said (though she had seen the flicker of apprehension in his face), 'You'll be back. What do you think you'll achieve?' That had been two years ago. She had resisted his pleas for her return, and her father's admonitions. In a few weeks the divorce by consent would be through, and that phase of her life would be at an end. She had not seen her husband or her father since the day she walked out.

In the old Morris Minor, Catherine said, 'We'll have to go, you know,' and Anna said, 'Where?', temporarily disorientated. Catherine made a derisory sound in her throat. 'You must have been dreaming. He told me how to get in – get evidence for the papers. Do you still have that security pass signed by your father?' Anna nodded, still half thinking of the divorce. They drove on through the rain.

Back at the camp that evening Catherine told one or two of the others about their conversation in the pub. The fire smoked heavily, fighting to gain a purchase on the damp wood. Most of the women had already gone to their tents, and the only light came from the guard-house almost a quarter of a mile away. 'Won't it be dangerous?' asked Josephine, the youngest member of the group. Her fair hair was untidily done up with a rubber band, and she carried her grubby baby on her hip. Nobody replied.

It was only two days later, when she and Catherine were actually driving down the road towards Porton Down, that Anna began to feel a little afraid. The demonstrations may have been uncomfortable, but they were, in the widest construction of the word, safe. Even the police, with their angry, irritated faces, had been part of the known structure of law and order. At worst there might be a few bruises, a fine, or a short spell in prison, but – even after all this time – the newspaper reporters and television cameras were never very far away. There had always been, even at the worst times, a sense of the rules, of behaviour within strained but acceptable limits. This was different. If the Russian was right, experiments were being conducted which the public knew nothing about. She glanced quickly at Catherine, hunched by her side in a fur-lined parka, but the other girl was sunk in her own thoughts, the beaked nose pointing straight at the windscreen and her eyes far away. Anna wished, just for a moment, that she had the courage to suggest they turn back. There was something sinister, twilit, about the world they were about to enter. Something beyond ordinary criminality: a place where it might not be fanciful to see death as a possible consequence of being caught. She wound the window up and turned the heater to full. The old car grumbled complainingly forward.

She was annoyed to find herself thinking about James. What she felt was more subtle than regret, or a sense of loss prompted by the memory of what it had been like at first. Such urgent passion, the constant need to touch, to stroke, to lay her cheek on his. For the first time since she had joined the group she felt uncertain. Believing still in the cause, she found herself suddenly resentful at what she had given up: a husband, a comfortable life, the prospect of children. It had seemed the right thing to do, then. Now, seeing the lines on her face, the first slackness of the flesh on her upper arms, she felt suddenly afraid. This was not a rehearsal, but the real thing. There would be no second chances soon, and she had begun to feel that she had used time she could ill afford in chasing chimeras and insubstantial dreams. Peering through the windscreen, she resolved that once this was over she would make her escape back to London. It would be possible then, because she would have done everything in her power to change opinions.

Night had shaded the landscape to drab grey and blacks by the time they arrived. The sullen sky still hurled rain down unceasingly, and the floor of the car had collected puddles from the leaks round the windscreen. Anna wished she had worn warmer clothing. She stopped the car in a lay-by and turned the engine off. By her side Catherine said urgently, 'No turning back. We must do it now,' and Anna took a deep breath and nodded, feeling that old childhood knot of fear in her stomach. She took the security pass from her pocket and gave it to Catherine. Her permissions had been withdrawn when she left, two years ago, but she knew that the department were not over-efficient. They could only try, after all. She found herself hoping that they wouldn't let her in. Guiltily she realized that if Catherine hadn't been with her she would have turned back.

She started the car. At the main gate she waited by the barrier while the guard walked across. He took the pass and scrutinized it for a moment, his eyes in shadow under the peaked hat. 'Your father isn't here, miss,' he said almost apologetically, and she smiled up at him with all the confidence she could muster. 'I know,' she said, cursing the tremor in her voice. 'We've come to see Professor Butterfield.' He still seemed uncertain until she said, with wild inventiveness. 'This is his niece from America. It's a surprise, you see.' The sergeant peered into the car for a moment and then smiled, handing back the pass. 'I shouldn't . . . but . . . all right,' and she smiled up at him like a trusting child.

It was just as the Russian had said it would be, Catherine whispered when they were inside. The long straight corridor. Past pathology on the right. Past forensic on the left. The lights blazed yellowly down the empty, lino-floored corridor.

From somewhere there was a distant humming and suddenly, as they passed an unmarked door, a telephone began to ring. They stood in silence for a moment, looking at each other, until it finally stopped. At the end of the corridor, just before a T-junction, Catherine caught Anna's arm and pointed. 'There,' she whispered triumphantly, 'just as he said.' The door was open and they went in.

Bergman lit the sergeant's cigarette and cupped his hand around the lighter flame to light his own. He was trying to give up, but it didn't seem the right time now. Not that it ever did. His face looked tired and drawn in the flickering light. Behind him Rivers stood massively, shifting from foot to foot, looking at the light in the entrance lobby. He can't wait to do it, Bergman thought, shuddering with distaste. The sergeant said, 'It was just as we were told, sir. We've been expecting them for a week.' He looked at Bergman oddly for a moment, turning away when the other man caught his eye.

Bergman looked at his watch. 'Time to go in, I suppose,' he said, and Rivers immediately began to walk towards the entrance. He moved with surprising speed for such a bulky man, his head thrust forward like a battering ram against the wind.

At the entrance Rivers took out his gun and screwed the silencer into place before putting it back in his pocket. They moved fast down the corridor, their rubber soles making no sound. The door at the end was open and Rivers walked in first, a few paces in front of Bergman. It all happened so quickly that the uncertain details teased at Bergman's mind for months afterwards. There were two figures standing by the animal cages, the taller of the two focusing a camera. In the cage a monkey cowered away from the bars, baring its teeth in a grotesque simulation of laughter. The second figure turned, and for an instant Bergman was caught, surprised to see her, hurt by her beauty. But it was too late, anyway. He had barely moved when Rivers' first shot caught her below the left breast and threw her against the wall. The other figure turned and Bergman saw a vision of her open mouth frozen in a silent scream. Then the face seemed to disintegrate and Catherine fell heavily. The camera dropped to the floor and the lens shattered.

Bergman leaned back against the wall, feeling his stomach heave. Nobody had identified the girls. Kagan had only said that Alexandrevitch had talked to a couple of girls. No descriptions. The lead had seemed so tenuous that Bergman had almost decided to check Rivers and himself out of the hotel and return to London by the time the call finally came. The caller had only referred to 'the two female subjects'. That was how the Bureau always dealt with these matters. It was easier without a human face, a human name. Bergman felt unreal, as though his limbs didn't belong to him.

Rivers surprised him, looking up from Catherine's body. 'We'll lug the guts into the other room.' It was a sudden, strange insight which deflected the grief for a moment. He would never have expected Rivers to read Shakespeare. He found himself saying in his mind, without conviction, 'It wasn't my fault. It's the job.' When Rivers had moved Catherine's body to the door he came back for Anna. Watching the other man, Bergman thought, I could kill him; but he only said, 'You make the report. Leave me here for a while,' ignoring Rivers' surprised glance. He knelt on the ground and turned her face towards the light. Her eyes were open, and she looked more worn, older than when he had last seen her. But still beautiful, he thought, and felt his eyes prickle. He felt at her throat, but there was no pulse at all. And there my lips have rested, and there.

Behind him, Rivers said: 'I wonder how soon before it gets into the papers?' Bergman said flatly, 'We've done our job. That's up to head office. They always get the clean end.'

5

When Avery's anonymous car nosed up the drive, Lydia, looking out of the bedroom window, felt a sudden return of the fears and thoughts she had half suppressed since his previous visit. For a few days her new perceptions had seemed to cut through the staleness of years, to set aside habit, the familiar actions and responses which she now saw made up the totality of her life with David. She had been acutely unhappy for days, unable to settle to anything for long, and wishing that the old familiar waters would close over their heads again so that she could shut away these painful new insights. The children, the familiar textures and colours of her home, even the new accommodations to David, all these made her wish this time past, even though the insights could never be forgotten. But the interview had underlined what she had begun to fear: that she had become only a habit for David. It seemed that the true springs of his action, the secret desires which lay at his core, fed elsewhere, beyond her reach. All this had remained with her, even after the other disquiets raised by Avery and his partner in their first visit had died to a dull, often revisited ache.

She pushed the window up and called to David. He had been working late at the House recently (and now she wondered about those evenings, too) and was taking a day off, stretched in a deck chair facing the sun. Even there, she noted ruefully, his briefcase was at his side and he was reading some papers.

'The two gentlemen I told you about are here.'

David got up from the chair as Avery walked across the grass towards him with his hand outstretched. Was she imagining it, or did David look worried? She turned away and tried to concentrate on preparing her shopping list.

Roger Burberry interested himself in the garden beds while Avery and David Marsh walked round the perimeter of the lawn. 'One day,' he thought, 'one day,' looking with envy at the deep beds of roses. It was like dreaming of winning the pools. However far he progressed (and he was realistic about his prospects) his pay from the department would never run to a Queen Anne mansion with rolling lawns and a Virginia creeper climbing strongly up its mellowed walls. He knew what Avery would be saying, and had an idea of the effect it would be having on David Marsh. But the likely consequences of the visit on Marsh and his family left Burberry unmoved. He had been a party to too many of these arrangements to view them with much sentiment. It was a philosophy inculcated by the department: that people were commodities, expendable in the interests of some greater good. His education had stopped short of any further consideration of the philosophical connotations of good and evil. He accepted that there were people above him in the department (lodged in the grey partitioned recesses of their headquarters in Central London) whose intimate relationship with the Almighty must qualify them to make such judgements. It was a comfortable abrogation of responsibility which left his mind free to concentrate on more enjoyable things. Gardening. Now there he prided himself on his expertise. When duties permitted he was always there at eight o'clock on the first day of the Chelsea

Flower Show. He would walk round with his pocket full of seeds (which never took), dreaming of owning a garden with a waterfall and baize-smooth grass.

Marsh and Avery had strolled back into earshot. Marsh was saying, 'This can be kept from my wife, can't it?' as by his side Avery paused to smell a rose, pulling it towards him with a white, brutal hand. 'That might be difficult. Most of the newspapers seem to key into the more interesting findings of my department.' He let the rose go and added unconvincingly, 'We've tried to plug the gaps, but you know how these things get out . . . ' He didn't try to give the other man any reassurance. Burberry could have told what was happening even without hearing the words. At these moments Avery always had an air of satisfaction.

They strolled past. Down by the willow they turned, and Burberry noted how Marsh unconsciously fell into step with the other man. With false concern, Avery said, 'Besides, it all really depends on what happens with this Russian character. The fact is that both you and he were clients of Sally Kane, and that constitutes a security risk. Remember Profumo . . . '

David said desperately, 'Please, if you can . . . ', putting his hand on Avery's sleeve. The bigger man stopped and looked down at his sleeve and then at Marsh, and the Minister dropped his hand and lowered his gaze. They came slowly back towards Burberry, and he joined them for the walk back to the house.

At the french windows Avery held out a hand. Ignoring Marsh's evident concern, he said, 'Nice to meet you, Mr Marsh,' with his menacing joviality. 'We'll probably want to talk to you again.'

Lydia looked down at her husband standing by the car. There seemed to be something craven in his attitude. As the car started to drive away she turned from the window quickly, in case David saw her. Now they would have to talk, and she felt suddenly afraid. They hadn't talked, really talked, for years. It might destroy what little was left.

Driving away, Avery talked to Burberry for a while. The sun slanted gently over a rippling cornfield to their right. Crows lazily flapped away from the road at their approach. When Avery had finished talking he drove in silence for a few minutes, handling the car with casual expertise. 'About time you started doing the newspaper briefings. You'd better get Sammy in tomorrow. And make sure you connect the story about the two girls. Nothing too obvious. We don't want to spell everything out.'

They drove in silence down the black road. Occasionally a tractor went past, or they were held up by an ancient car taking its country time down the middle of the road. Burberry started to daydream about David Marsh's garden. Perhaps he and Elsa could move somewhere larger with a patch of garden. He felt happier than he had for weeks.

6

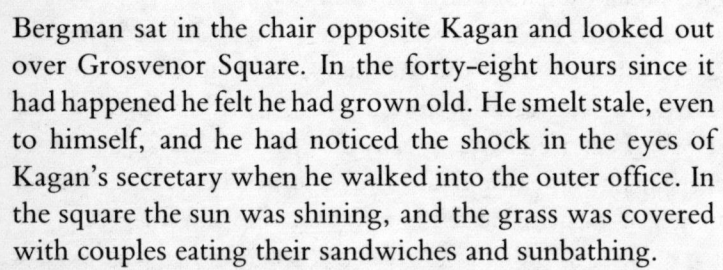

Bergman sat in the chair opposite Kagan and looked out over Grosvenor Square. In the forty-eight hours since it had happened he felt he had grown old. He smelt stale, even to himself, and he had noticed the shock in the eyes of Kagan's secretary when he walked into the outer office. In the square the sun was shining, and the grass was covered with couples eating their sandwiches and sunbathing.

Kagan finished his call and put the receiver down. He looked like a Viennese butcher, with his florid face, his varicosed nose and the thinning ginger hair which he dragged over his bald patch from behind his right ear. His stomach bulged over the waistline of his blue trousers and his crumpled shirt had sweat stains under the arms. He looked, as always, acutely uncomfortable.

He folded his freckled, pudgy hands under his arms, then smelt the fingers of his right hand. Even in his misery James felt a shuddering distaste. Kagan never cared how he looked to anyone else. He even picked his nose in public, gazing at the mucus under his fingernail with fascination before flicking it away.

Kagan said, 'Look, it was just one of those crazy coincidences. The police tipped us off that two women were staying at the pub. We set it up for Alexandrevitch . . . ' He gestured helplessly, and rocked the chair back. 'I know it must be tough about Anna but, after all, you hadn't seen her for a couple of years. Look at it in the wider sense. What better to convince the Russkies? Even Kalevsky will believe this one. And that makes Alexandrevitch's job much easier.'

Bergman felt a bitter taste in his mouth. He took his handkerchief out and wiped it across his forehead, fighting to stay calm. Kagan was on his third wife. How could he comprehend what it meant to be separated from the person you loved, to be involved in this? In that corridor, before he had known about Anna, only that it was 'two female subjects', he had momentarily thought of aborting the mission. But he had thought, then, of the aim of the operation. (When Maskelyne was giving them a skeleton briefing on the British end, he had said, 'Above all personal considerations, we must recognize that total success in this venture will pave the way for those who follow to make this world a safer place in the future for our children': the irony of which had struck Bergman several times.) He had reflected since that he had only raised a token objection when he was informed that the targets would be women. It had seemed, then, like some bad joke which, once told, could be forgotten, and the reality had returned only briefly as he walked up the corridor behind Rivers. (The psychologist in Basic Training had said casually, almost conversationally, 'We'll teach you the art of denial so that if you were ordered to, you could kill your own mother.')

But this time he had been unable to come to terms. This grief, which drove sleep away, which tormented him with memories of their times together, which recollected the precise textures of her skin and hair, seemed to grow daily. When Anna had gone to Greenham, Maskelyne had said, 'I have no daughter,' smiling his brief, humourless rictus. And James, too, had felt instantly dispossessed of her and was suddenly aware of the tenuousness of human relationships once habit had gone. He had not seen Anna since that day until he had briefly seen her face as she turned to meet her death. He had never, could never, possess Maskelyne's total certitude. Three days after she had gone James had met Maskelyne at the club, and Maskelyne had said, 'I've changed my will. She will get nothing, now.' It was how he worked. James wasn't even sure that Maskelyne would know of her death. The neutral report which had been courtesy-copied to Maskelyne only referred to 'the female subjects'.

Kagan was saying, 'We mustn't push too hard. You know that the English always want an official inquiry with all the facts published once things go beyond a certain stage.' He put his hands behind his head and tilted his chair again, looking up at the ceiling. 'Now that's something we'd find it hard to fix. Any other touches would be overkill. We'll have to leave it to Kalevsky's boys to figure out the connections.' He looked at Bergman quizzically, and the other man nodded.

'Has the Brigadier been officially informed, sir?'

'Hell, no,' Kagan said. He seemed genuinely shocked by the query. 'You saw the report. Besides, you know he had cut off all contact with her since she started this Greenham nonsense . . . ' He looked shrewdly at Bergman for a moment, narrowing his eyes. 'And you weren't exactly on the phone with her yourself, were you.'

In his mind Bergman screamed, 'No, but this is too much.' He turned in his chair as though the physical movement might blot out the picture of Anna as he had last seen her: and other pictures and sensations – the secluded beach on their honeymoon, the taste of her hair in his mouth. With an effort he pulled himself back to the present, surprised to find he could speak so calmly. 'I see that Avery's boys kept her name out of the papers?' His voice rose inquiringly.

Kagan nodded, shaking his head in admiration. 'That was one of his touches. Kalevsky will find out who she is, of course. But as we deliberately haven't made any capital out of it, any suspicions he might have should be allayed.'

'So Maskelyne might never know?'

'Possibly.' The subject had lost interest for Kagan. 'Who knows?' The telephone rang again and Kagan put his hand over it. 'By the way, Jimmy, I've arranged for you to take a month off. Take in a few shows, get away.' He waved an expansive arm towards the office window and picked up the receiver.

When James got into the corridor he hesitated, half turning back. He hadn't asked about the funeral. Then he remembered that Avery's rat-like partner had told him with a smile that she had been 'put down' anonymously in a cemetery in Salisbury. Because Avery didn't want it spelt out in the papers, they didn't want any company operatives or traceable contacts there.

He walked diagonally across the square towards Brook Street. He felt alienated from the people in the square, remote. Perhaps he should carry a bell and cry, 'Unclean! Unclean!'

7

Avery phoned through the news to the club from a callbox. Bergman was having an uneasy drink with Maskelyne, and the call came as a welcome diversion after half an hour's discussion of trivia with his father-in-law, wondering, while they talked idly, whether or not the other man knew what had happened. Typical of Maskelyne to call him in to verify file details to close out the German operation: it was something he could have done quite easily on his own. He vented his pent-up tension on Avery.

'You shouldn't have called here on an open phone . . . If the Brigadier had taken this call you'd be for the high jump.'

The voice at the other end of the phone held a genuine hint of panic. 'You'd better get down here immediately. The wife is in a terrible state. He's dead . . . yes, I'm sure. There was a note but she hasn't let us see it. She's talking about going to the press.' There was a silence, and James could hear the wind complaining in the wires. Far away there was the crackle of other voices carrying on an indistinguishable conversation. Avery said, 'There's bound to be an inquiry.'

Bergman said, 'Keep everything contained. We'll be on our way.' Walking back through the lobby to rejoin Maskelyne, he wondered gloomily how Kagan would react. Still, no one could have foreseen this. The thought didn't convince him, and he knew it wouldn't convince Kagan. He found himself surprised, again, at his coldness. It seemed the only way he could cope at present. Putting a distance between himself and others. He'd met Marsh and Lydia at official functions several times, and had quite liked them. Yet, strangely enough considering his own recent experience, it seemed difficult to think himself into Lydia's predicament.

It was the first time he had ever seen Maskelyne angry. 'The bloody fool,' he said vehemently. 'We'd better go at once.' They walked in silence to the car park in Cork Street. A gusty wind hurled paper and rubbish down the pavement, and Bergman felt his eyes smarting from the fine grit. He felt ashamed, again, to see the reflection of Maskelyne's dehumanization in himself. Marsh had done something inconvenient. It would create a problem in the grand strategy devised by Kagan and Maskelyne which would have to be worked out. They drove in silence, each preoccupied with their own thoughts. As they neared Marsh's home Maskelyne said, as though it were the continuation of some interrupted conversation between them, 'I'll persuade them to nominate Joseph Sainsbury if there's to be an inquiry.'

James was surprised. He'd seen Sainsbury in the distance at Reinecke's cocktail party and had read a number of articles about him in the press over the years. Sainsbury was a man he connected more with such bodies as the Arts Council, appeals for the Tate. One of the articles had suggested that he had spent more time during his latter years in helping charities than in working for the partnership he had built up. He had a reputation for probity, and a keen brain. Nothing about him seemed to suggest that he was an obvious candidate to serve the department's needs.

He said cautiously, 'That seems an odd choice, if you don't mind my saying so, sir.'

Maskelyne pulled the car to a halt on the gravelled drive

of Marsh's house. Marsh's car was parked outside the garage and Avery's sat just behind it. Darkness had begun to fall and a light came on in the hall. With the air of a man whose mind is made up, Maskelyne said, 'Joseph was my ADC in the war. He has a very strong sense of duty and patriotism. They couldn't pick anyone better.'

Lydia was sitting in the hall, weeping hysterically. Mrs Baines stood awkwardly by her side with an arm around her shoulders. The two boys stood, open-mouthed, by the other side of the chair, shifting awkwardly from foot to foot as they watched Bergman and Maskelyne with round, bemused eyes. Avery came through the kitchen at the back, followed by his partner. He indicated that they should climb the stairs, and the three of them followed Maskelyne up to the landing. 'He's in there,' Avery said in a sepulchral whisper, as though he were in a cathedral.

James was quite unprepared for the sight. Marsh lay in the bath fully clad in a shirt that had been white and grey flannels. The sides of the yellow enamel ran with red runnels, and his left arm hung limply over the side with a deep cut in the wrist. Some drops of blood had fallen on to the peach-coloured carpet. His face lay against the edge of the bath, livid, pushed into a grin of inane fixity by the pressure of the bath rim. Maskelyne stood over the figure, looking down impassively. 'The Roman way,' he said softly. James felt his stomach heave. He had just reached the basin in time to vomit. He wiped his mouth, and caught Avery looking at him in the mirror with a slight smile on his face. 'Not so tough, eh?' the smile seemed to be saying.

The front doorbell rang, and they could hear the door being opened, followed by the sound of Mrs Baines' distressed voice. 'You can't go up . . . ' she said, and then there was the sound of heavy footsteps coming up the stairs.

Avery said hurriedly, 'It was bound to get out, sir. So I

got on to Sammy. At least we have a chance of containing the story.'

The photographer started to line up his camera, one foot on the plinth on which the bath rested. Maskelyne moved fast, chopping his forearm down across the man's arms with brutal force, so that the camera fell to the carpet. 'No photographs,' he said, his voice languid and deceptively conversational. 'No briefing, either. Not until we've had a chance to find out what's happened. We'll contact you, don't worry.' When the photographer had gone, escorted by Burberry, Maskelyne turned to Avery.

'That's your second mistake, Mr Avery. The first was evidently your original interrogation. We can't afford too many of those, you know.' Bergman felt a mean sense of revenge, watching the big man fight to keep his anxiety under control.

In the drawing-room Maskelyne sat next to Lydia with a sympathetic arm around her shoulder. Avery and his partner followed the boys through the french windows into the garden. Bergman sat in the spoon-backed chair in the corner, awkwardly nursing a whisky Mrs Baines had poured him. He reached in his pocket for his cigarettes and then remembered Marsh had disliked the habit with all the fervour of the ex-smoker. He listened to Maskelyne with unwilling admiration. It was not untinged with a feeling akin to horror – that the man who had effectively brought about her husband's death should seem so solicitous of Lydia's welfare. Not that she knew anything of the dark complicities which had led to this, he reflected. From her mumbled responses he gathered that Marsh had felt guilty about his liaison with Sally Kane, and had felt unable to face the publicity, the degradation.

She was saying, 'I still can't believe it . . . if only I could have helped . . .', and Maskelyne sighed with apparent sympathy. 'It will take time to come to terms with what has happened. But there was nothing you could do. Nothing at all.'

Bergman sipped his whisky. Something about Lydia reminded him of Anna, and he wondered again if Maskelyne knew what had happened. Sharp and unexpected, the memory of his first meeting with Anna returned.

It had been five years ago. Maskelyne's wife, Julia, had died quite suddenly and unexpectedly of a heart attack. When the news had come through, Bergman had been in Berlin, temporarily on secondment to Maskelyne. He had spent weeks of frustration, mainly engaged in low-level investigations of army and UN personnel. The reverberations of the case of Willy Brandt's secretary had flushed a sheaf of over-reactions into the in-tray in the small suite of offices he shared with Maskelyne. Judith, Maskelyne's sensible, thirty-year-old secretary who fancied herself a bit in love with Bergman, used to smile sympathetically as she refilled his in-tray. 'Perhaps something big will come along soon,' she would say teasingly, resting her hand on his shoulder for a moment as she leaned forward to put his coffee cup on the desk. Bergman had taken her out once or twice – to Axel's Keller or the Tourment d'Amour – but something about her pink-and-white wholesomeness deterred him. They held hands once, walking in the shadow of the Wall, but it was for the mutual comfort of two people far from home.

Then the big thing had come from an unexpected quarter. The news of Julia's death. When the telegram came Maskelyne had held it for a few moments, gazing out of the window with the air of a man who could not, for the moment, believe what he had just read. Something in the stillness had told James that this was serious. Maskelyne had said something to himself, softly, as though he were alone, as though in confirmation. It sounded like a name. Two days later they were in Surrey. Kagan had once told

James that Maskelyne had 'what the Limeys call "family money"', but James had been unprepared for the setting. The Georgian house stood amidst rolling lawns and well-stocked shrubberies. In the middle distance, far below the furthest terraces, the Pilgrim's Way scarred the chalk swell of the slope, and beyond, the gentle hills lay in blue haze.

The mourners all seemed to be titled (or, at least, what Anna used later to call, 'county, my dear'), and James had noticed that their funeral clothes were shiny and, in some cases, ill-repaired, that the cars were ancient Daimlers and even older Rolls-Royces. But they all had in common an indefinable air of superiority: the same air which had at first amused him with George Maskelyne, and had then diminished him, drip by drip.

He had felt awkward, sipping an unaccustomed dry sherry, feeling conspicuous in his squarely cut grey suit amidst the black of all the other mourners. Anna had come across to him at the wake and he had immediately, forcefully, been struck by her beauty. He remembered her first words, delivered *sotto voce* as she gestured towards her father. 'A branch of the family ran a Hall of Magic in Piccadilly at the turn of the century. Daddy's a little theatrical too, don't you think?' He had felt momentarily embarrassed by her flippancy, feeling it to be out of place here. But it had been only fleeting, one facet of the myriad separate people she seemed to be. At first it was the elusiveness itself that caught him, seeming, in its very vagueness, to permit his fantasies about her to burgeon. It was only later that he began to realize the neurotic psychopathology which lay beneath it. She had a chameleon quality which played to the gallery of those surrounding her. 'Aren't you different with different people?' she had mocked him once, as though his apparently stable personality was to be derided.

The two boys walking into the circle of light outside the

house on the patio broke his uneasy reverie. Burberry was saying, 'Very interesting . . . ' in an unconvincing way, in response to something the younger boy had said. Maskelyne stood up and said, 'We'll make the arrangements, Mrs Marsh. And please accept my deepest condolences. I'll leave a man here, if I may, until the police are finished, and Mr Avery here will run you over to your sister's house.'

James saw Lydia Marsh look at Avery and said, without thinking, 'Let me do that, sir. Perhaps Mr Avery will give you a lift back, and I'll return the car to the club car park tomorrow, if that's all right?' Lydia shot him a grateful glance, and he knew that his instinct had been right.

Maskelyne hesitated for a moment and then said, 'Check,' pursing his lips. James knew him well enough to know that he was angry.

In the car Lydia sat silent with her hands in her lap, looking out at the grey-black topography of the bushes and trees speeding past the window. Once or twice she indicated a direction in response to James's questioning. Glancing sideways, he could just make out her features in the green glow from the dashboard lights. Grief, pain, had temporarily drawn fine lines around her mouth, had given the eyes a tearful, wrinkled pouchiness.

A couple of miles outside Maidenhead she said in a detached, little-girl voice, 'Could we stop and have a drink?' A few hundred yards further down, James turned off the road into the car park of a thatched pub. 'I suddenly felt thirsty,' she said by way of an explanation, smiling up briefly at him as he opened the door for her. Walking in, she stumbled slightly, leaning against him for a moment. Seeing his concern she smiled and said, 'I feel all right, really. Just a bit shaky, that's all.'

They sat in a corner of the long saloon bar room, at a diagonal extremity from the only other couple in the room.

An ancient Alsatian walked dysphasically to look for food, twitched its nose at the table while James patted his head, and moved away. 'Sorry,' Lydia said, wry-mouthed, putting down her glass, and James said softly, 'Hey. No need to apologize. You've had a tough ride.' He bought another couple of drinks, ignoring her protests, thinking that this might be the best thing to relax her. And she began to talk, at first haltingly, pausing while she assessed what she could and couldn't say, glancing towards him from time to time, and then more freely, as though he had known her and David for a long time, was an old friend. Of how it had been at first, the punt on the Backs under the trailing willow after the May Ball, and the plans to change priorities, to create a new Utopia, of the dreams and strength of their youth. 'Tell me,' he said when she faltered, describing how the changes had begun, the insidiousness of ambition, and felt, for just a moment, that she was betraying a loyalty. And later, when she had paused again, it was strong enough between them for him to say (remembering Anna), 'The important thing is never to lie to yourself, never to paint false pictures, for then you stop growing, remain caught,' and he had almost, though not quite, begun to tell her about Anna. When, finally, she put up her hands to her face and started to weep, he held her dark head against his shoulder and stroked her hair, while the landlord smiled at him, fleetingly, sympathetically, and then looked away.

In the car again she was quiet, with an easy silence. Twice she touched his arm and indicated where he should turn. From the corner of his eye James could see her slender hands resting quietly in her lap. He felt a confusion of feelings: a hope that he had thought lost for ever; a sense of guilt that he should be so aware of Lydia that he felt raw with the secret knowledge of what really happened.

Later, as they drew up in front of her sister's house, Lydia said wonderingly, 'I can't thank you enough. I feel as if

I've known you for years,' and James smiled at her, letting himself out to hold the door open for her. Standing, awkward for a moment, he said, 'I'll call you sometime. It helps to talk . . . ', not daring to ask if that was all right. He had breathed a deep inward sigh of relief when she nodded as though, of course, that was understood, that it almost didn't need to be said. He turned the car on the sweep of gravel and, when he saw the door open and a woman step out into the porch and embrace Lydia, he put the headlights on full beam and drove slowly down the drive, wondering, suddenly, exactly where he was.

8

Sir Joseph Sainsbury sat down gratefully in the leather chair. He had always retained a child's wonder about machinery of any kind. The X-ray machine which stood in one corner, the array of instruments on Andre Sheyrer's desk, all possessed a comforting and slightly alien mystique. This was an area so far outside his own sphere of competence that he felt temporarily and comfortingly restored to the role of a trusting child. And, to his secret amusement, even Andre, one of his closest friends and a regular bridge and dinner-party partner, took on some slightly pompous Wimpole Street mannerisms in his consulting room. After the warm greeting his manner had become crisp and professional, the questioning terse and oddly objective. Bowel movements, indeed, Joseph thought, briefly aware of the curious role one's professional life sometimes conferred upon one in the presence of friends.

Andre consulted his notes on the other side of the desk while Joseph, released for the moment from his usual pressing round of engagements, sat and ruminated. It was a mode of thinking which had begun to grow disproportionate of late. He chided himself about the indulgence of it which ran so counter to the work ethic of his upbringing. But it was undeniably pleasant, and he permitted himself these small forays into memory from time to time.

They made a strangely contrasting pair. Sheyrer small, with a weather-worn skin, and paling auburn hair grizzling to white at the temples. Sainsbury, grotesquely obese, with the heavy, deceptively misleading features of a stupid man. They had known each other since Balliol, almost fifty years before, when they both got firsts – Andre in medicine and Joseph in law. There had always been a playful rivalry between them which had threatened to develop into something more serious when Joseph got his baronetcy, but their friendship was too deeply rooted for any permanent malice to prevail. It was, in common with most of Joseph's friendships, more at home in the club, or in the ambience of an occasional lunch or dinner. It had an essential maleness about it which sat uneasily with family dinner parties or domestic occasions.

Outside the consulting-room windows the sun drenched the pastel wall on the opposite side of Wimpole Street. It was hot for May, and Joseph mopped his forehead with a tissue, watching his friend working on his notes. It was strange to feel in this subordinate position. He was so accustomed to controlling all the situations in which he was involved, to being the expert to whom all others looked for an opinion or a judgement. Though he suspected that the prognosis confirmed his own inner conviction, watching his friend's frown as Andre made his notes, it was still pleasant to relax, to know that for once there was nothing he could contribute.

He shifted in his chair and Sheyrer looked at him over the gold-rimmed half glasses.

'Well, my friend, it doesn't look too good, I'm afraid . . . ' He put his elbows on the desk, and his fingers together to form a pyramid, looking down at the papers in front of him. Joseph found himself wryly amused at his friend's embarrassment.

'You know me, Andre. I prefer the truth to medical equivocation or deceptive prognoses. Tell me simply. How long?'

Why did people have to move around, to pick things up and put them down, when they were under stress? Joseph had removed himself, as had been his habit since the war, to a place beyond fear or involvement where he could view whatever had happened with the detached irony which had become so characteristic of him.

Andre stood at the window with his back to his friend. When he spoke his voice sounded muffled. Tears, perhaps, Joseph wondered. He composed himself for the worst.

'Elaine once asked me to look after you when she had gone. Persuade you to lose some weight, stop drinking brandy, take holidays. Fine friend I've turned out to be . . . '

Joseph said gently, 'You are not your brother's keeper. Besides, I would never have listened. You know that . . . ' It must be very serious, he thought.

Andre walked back and stood behind the desk, looking down at his friend.

'I wouldn't dream of trying to deceive you. Your heart is very damaged. It could really be any time but, with care, a year or so. I'm afraid there is nothing to be done.' A tear slid down under the frame of the eyeglasses and he wiped it away with an angry gesture.

'There is no need for tears,' Joseph said, putting his tie round his neck and beginning to fasten it with slow, deliberate movements of his great hands, 'it comes to us all. And three-score years and ten is my allowance, after all.' In one part of his mind he was calculating, already, the disposal of his directorships, the redispositions of his will, and who might be able to take over the chairmanship of his charitable commissions. It was hard when you had no children. He reflected, with grim humour, that some of his younger partners might not be too upset at the news.

At the door he patted his friend's shoulder gently. 'Don't take it personally, Andre. I have lived as I wanted to and here are the consequences. That's all.'

They arranged to meet for a rubber of bridge later in the week. 'Be careful,' Sheyrer warned anxiously, and Joseph smiled at him, amused by this prayer for the dying from the physician. He felt strangely touched to see his friend's helplessness in the face of mortality.

And this is how it will be from now on, he thought, smiling at a worried-looking woman with a young child as he walked down the stairs. The irrational feeling of immortality, the childlike idea that disasters always happened to someone else – these comforting illusions had suddenly gone.

Walking down Wimpole Street towards Cavendish Square, he felt lonely. He had sent the car away, partly suspecting that he might need to be alone in order to recover his composure. As he walked he was conscious of his heart pumping, and the needle-like pains behind his breastbone which had finally brought him to Andre for the check-up had begun again. Using his customary specific against fear and loneliness, he forced himself to think. He walked through a crowd of heavily veiled Arab women, waiting by their chauffeur-driven limousines, oblivious of their presence.

Even now there was one thing he felt reluctant to give up. Two days previously he had accepted an invitation to have a drink with George Maskelyne at the club. Knowing George, he had realized immediately that this was no mere social engagement. Over the years he had played bridge with George, had attended Julia's funeral, and Anna's wedding to that young American . . . what was his name? But he had never credited George with a casual social life in the ordinary sense of the word. Everything George did was calculated, and Joseph had long since concluded that George valued mechanisms and abstract ideals far more than flesh and blood. On the rare occasions George had spoken with his dry passion, Joseph had remained silent, hugging to himself his own belief that such attitudes, such ideals, had served their purpose during that long and bitter war but had an archaic inappropriateness in times of peace. But one thing he did know. It must be serious.

They had met in one of the private rooms the club reserved for conferences. The faint hum from the early diners in the rooms below was almost inaudible. Joseph gratefully accepted the large whisky George had poured him. Sitting in the comfortable armchair he listened, head on hand, to the story Maskelyne had to tell.

George started by talking about Marsh's death (which Joseph had, of course, read about in the papers). One of the rags, George said with uncharacteristic venom, had made a connection between David Marsh's death and a picture of Marsh taken at a party with Sally Kane. Marsh had access to certain classified information, the dissemination of which could affect the outcome of the forthcoming SALT talks. And, it appeared, another client of Sally Kane, and a regular at Marsh's parties, had been one Pyotr Dmitri Alexandrevitch. He showed Joseph a photograph of Gorbachev, Gromyko and other prominent CCCP members, pointing to a figure in the second row. 'That's him, taken at the May Day Parade.'

'What are the terms of reference?' Sainsbury asked, and Maskelyne said neutrally, 'One can only hope that the eventual verdict might be that Marsh couldn't face the facts of his liaison with Sally Kane becoming public knowledge. His wife had been devastated by the news . . . '

'What are the terms of reference?' Sainsbury asked patiently again, and Maskelyne shot him a hard, level look.

'The nature of the information to which Marsh had access must never be divulged. Even to you, Joseph.'

To Sainsbury's surprise, George reached out and put a hand on his shoulder. In all the years I've known him I've never known him to do that, Joseph thought.

'I'm not the man if you need a whitewash,' he said warningly, and Maskelyne nodded.

'But you are a man who knows how the world works, and how important national security is. And you know that the truth can be presented in such a way as to safeguard such principles.'

There was something here that Joseph didn't like. Impossible to put his finger on it. He had a niggling sense that there was something unclean, underhand, at the bottom of all this. He sighed. It had all the characteristics that intrigued him. A tantalizing incompleteness. A sense, conveyed by Maskelyne's deliberate choice of words, of some government department's complicity.

'One condition,' he said. 'That my findings are published in full. No editorial control.'

Maskelyne hesitated fractionally and then nodded. 'We'll do it through HMSO,' he said, and they shook hands on it and walked their separate ways. The next day all the national dailies had carried the news, with the usual flattering hyperbole and a twenty-year-old picture George must have given them.

In Cavendish Square he sat on a bench. A pair of lovers lay on the grass a few feet away, engrossed in each other. 'Lie on top of me,' the girl whispered, and the youth's head came up uncertainly, looking around the crowded square. Joseph watched a slim girl walk past. She had a short red skirt, and crimson sandals over her bare feet. He watched her abstractedly, wondering if he had the strength to carry out the inquiry. 'Oh God. Give me time,' he said, standing up. The woman at the other end of the bench watched him warily. She'd noticed a lot of people talking to themselves. Perhaps it was living in London that did it to people.

9

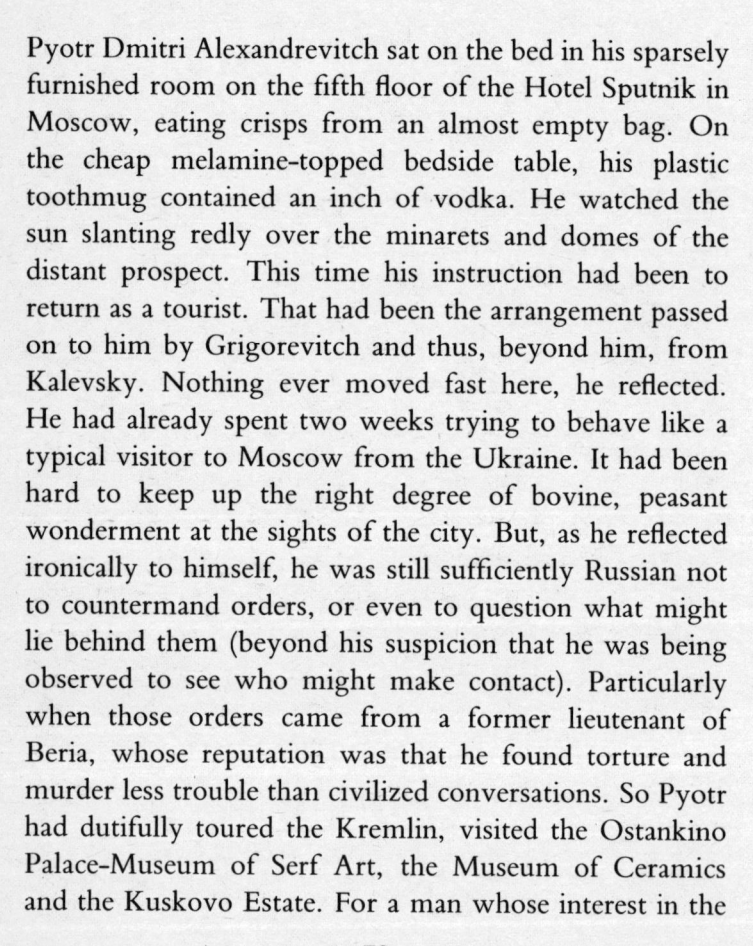

Pyotr Dmitri Alexandrevitch sat on the bed in his sparsely furnished room on the fifth floor of the Hotel Sputnik in Moscow, eating crisps from an almost empty bag. On the cheap melamine-topped bedside table, his plastic toothmug contained an inch of vodka. He watched the sun slanting redly over the minarets and domes of the distant prospect. This time his instruction had been to return as a tourist. That had been the arrangement passed on to him by Grigorevitch and thus, beyond him, from Kalevsky. Nothing ever moved fast here, he reflected. He had already spent two weeks trying to behave like a typical visitor to Moscow from the Ukraine. It had been hard to keep up the right degree of bovine, peasant wonderment at the sights of the city. But, as he reflected ironically to himself, he was still sufficiently Russian not to countermand orders, or even to question what might lie behind them (beyond his suspicion that he was being observed to see who might make contact). Particularly when those orders came from a former lieutenant of Beria, whose reputation was that he found torture and murder less trouble than civilized conversations. So Pyotr had dutifully toured the Kremlin, visited the Ostankino Palace-Museum of Serf Art, the Museum of Ceramics and the Kuskovo Estate. For a man whose interest in the arts was limited it had been an extremely fatiguing two weeks. Occasionally, surrounded by bluff Americans and enthusiastic English, he had even wondered at the wisdom of the choice he had made, but he knew from long experience that for him the excitement had always been the daily uncertainty of the double life he led. Certainly, he thought again, as he had so many times before, looking at the dowdy room with its cheap furniture, it was nothing to do with money.

On the second day he had become aware of them. Two figures in the grey, ill-cut suits of the service. Kalevsky's men, undoubtedly. They had made no effort to hide themselves, walking quite openly behind him when he was on foot, or following his rented Moskvich in a black Zil with smoked glass. He knew how Kalevsky worked. He could expect a visit any time within the next few days. He crumpled the crisp packet and tossed it into the bin, draining the last drops of his vodka with a sigh. The previous occupant had left a tattered edition of *Krokodil*, and he flicked idly through the pages, half his attention focused on the interview ahead.

The knock on the door was brisk and peremptory. Before Pyotr had time to clear his throat and call, 'Come in,' the door opened and a small man with flat, brutal features came through it, followed by a taller, square-shouldered man who closed the door softly behind him. As he got off the bed to greet them Pyotr realized that the smaller man was Oleg Grishkin who had been in his year at the university. Kalevsky was certainly treating this seriously to send his deputy along, he thought, feeling a tremor of fear in his stomach. Grishkin's speciality had been counter-propaganda, placing agents, and briefings. Alexandrevitch knew, too, that the rumours of dissidents whose constitutions had been too frail to cope with his robust techniques of persuasion had often been true. He would have to be careful.

Grishkin ignored Pyotr's outstretched hand, and motioned him to sit on the bed. The other man took up a position by the door, legs slightly apart, hands folded over his crutch. Standard KGB stance, Alexandrevitch thought. He felt uneasy, now that the interview for which he had so long prepared was finally taking place. Had Kagan and Maskelyne and all those faceless men beyond them really done their job properly? Not that there could be any turning back now, in any event. He would have to rely on Kalevsky's people in the West to put all the pieces together. It had seemed a good idea to leave those pieces unassembled when he had discussed the matter in the London office (was that only six weeks ago?). Now he was not so sure.

Grishkin sat on the chair, legs apart, his elbows resting on his thighs and his hands hanging down. He leaned forward confidentially and spoke softly, so softly that the man at the door could not hear. And no microphones, Alexandrevitch thought. That must mean something.

'Who gave you authority to join the General Secretary on the podium, Comrade?'

So it was to be the soft approach. This was an easy one.

'You know that there is always one place for a member of our Embassy staff from Britain. Our Comrade Ambassador has always been fair in allocating this place to people who have a long service record. This year it was my turn.'

Grishkin gave him a hard look, and then looked down at his hand. He nodded slightly, in what could have been taken as a gesture of assent, and looked up again.

'Pyotr Alexandrevitch. We understand you may have news which could be of interest in connection with the forthcoming talks in Geneva.'

Pyotr's palms felt damp and he rubbed them surreptitiously over the coarse fabric of the coverlet.

'Comrade,' he said, and was surprised to find that his voice sounded normal. 'The news I have is not precise and documented. You know about Marsh and the girl and the Commission of Inquiry and what the Western press have been saying . . . ' He paused, and Grishkin inclined his head fractionally, though the flat gaze of his black eyes never left Alexandrevitch's face. The man by the door moved his feet and coughed once, managing to inject a note of apology into the sound.

'You know that the girl told me that there was something happening at the Government Research Establishment at Porton Down which seemed to be creating excitement. Our people have known of the military nature of much of the work done there for over a decade now. And you know about the girls I used to try to find out what was happening . . . ' From the corner of his eye he saw the red light of the sun finally fade over Grishkin's shoulder, suffusing the minarets in a soft grey and pink dusk. He wondered if the other man knew that one of those girls was Maskelyne's daughter. He cursed Avery. It had been Avery's idea to separate the news items so that Kalevsky's people would have to put everything together for themselves. More authentic, he had argued. It was all right for him, dealing with the safe end of the operation in England.

Grishkin made a dismissive movement with his hand. Now there was no trace of politeness in his tone, and Alexandrevitch fancied that the man at the door looked more menacing, too. 'You know how things work here. In three weeks the talks begin again in Geneva. We are concerned about the build-up in Europe, the Cruise sitings in Britain and the Pershings in Germany, and we need to have precise information about the position of the

Western Alliance. We will probably trade off on the short-range missiles. The Warsaw Pact level is such that we do not need extra strength in Europe. But it is the overall picture we need to evaluate. We have all the American information we need. We can almost rely upon their newspapers to supply us with that . . . ' His voice sounded contemptuous. He raised a forefinger and wagged it towards Pyotr. 'But the British are different. What is the French reference? Perfidious Albion. Their so-called "open society" is a myth. They seem to have developed something, but what exactly . . . ' He let the speech trail into an interrogative silence.

Sometimes, Alexandrevitch thought, sometimes the strain becomes too much. In the mirror over the handbasin he caught sight of his face. Grey, wispy hair surmounting a pallid, drawn face: pouches under the eyes, and pronounced brackets round the mouth. He could point the connection no further to Grishkin. Perhaps Grishkin did know about the girls, but he couldn't be sure. He looked at the other man, uncertain of what to say next.

Abruptly Grishkin got up.

'What was the Kane girl like in bed?' he asked, his eyes suddenly speculative with prurient curiosity.

Alexandrevitch felt an immediate release of tension in his stomach. The worst was over. He forced a man-to-man joviality into his voice. 'Just like the whores in Leningrad. You know, Comrade, very willing but no heart.'

Grishkin looked at him for a moment and then walked to the door. The other man opened it deferentially, and Grishkin paused for a moment with his hand on the door handle and said, 'You'd better stay for a few days. We'll need to talk to you again.' He indicated the other man.

'If you need anything, you'll always find Viktor somewhere close by.'

Pyotr held his smile until the door closed. He was sure Viktor would always know where to find him. Suddenly he felt in a sprung trap. They had always told him that you were alone, those grey men in London. Then it had seemed like a sentimental philosophical tenet. Now for the first time he knew it to be true. He poured himself another vodka and lay on the bed. He was very, very frightened.

10

Kagan was in the seat next to Senator Reinecke. That was one of the downside factors to his job, he reflected philosophically. The plane had sat on the tarmac at Heathrow for twenty minutes, waiting for clearance to Geneva. Behind them, in the body of the plane on the other side of the curtain, sat the rest of the negotiating team, and behind them again, that phalanx of grim-faced, prematurely old, anonymous faces bedecked with dark glasses which accompanied Reinecke everywhere. ('Even to the door of the fucking john,' Reinecke had complained sourly to Kagan once.)

Reinecke was a lean, tense, profane man of fifty or so. Nobody would credit his athletic record at Yale now, seeing him puff his way through fifty Chesterfield a day. But that energy had not dissipated, merely changed direction. By thirty he had achieved his goal of building up a successful electronics company, which left him free to pursue his career in politics. He had been a Republican senator for eight years now, though – unadmitted to anyone else – he had fallen behind in his self-imposed schedule towards the achievement of his ultimate ambition. But that was still possible, if he pulled this off. He rarely contemplated the possibility of failure, but if he didn't succeed there was a long and honourable list of people who had failed at the same game. His staff found him frighteningly well informed, and as unsparing of them as he was of himself.

He put out his cigarette and half turned towards Kagan. 'I've heard that James Bergman has been drinking a little. I hope you're keeping an eye on him . . .' Kagan wondered again where the Senator got his information. He himself had been keeping tabs on Bergman. He knew about the visits to La Valbonne, the argument with the bouncer, the two-bottle sessions in the Chopper Lump in the company of a blonde lady. He had decided to leave things for a while, confident that Bergman's essential toughness would reassert itself. To some extent it was a matter of personal pride. He had chosen Bergman and two others from the pre-'Nam training course, and they had worked out just fine so far. The course had given them the right emotional attitudes: no commitments which overrode the department's interests, kill or be killed, total loyalty. Hell, he could tolerate a little deviation when a man had done a good tour of duty.

Aloud he said, 'One of the girls was his ex-wife, sir. He didn't know until Rivers had done the job right in front of him.'

Reinecke turned further in his seat to look at Kagan in disbelief. 'Christ,' he said disgustedly, 'you boys are really something else. Your top operative doesn't know the woman he's instructed to waste is his ex-wife. You expect me to believe that?'

The plane started to taxi forward, and muted muzak began to be piped into the cabin. Kagan managed to keep a satisfied smile from his face. He'd thought about this carefully, knowing that Reinecke would find out the facts. At least here he knew there was an adequate defence.

'That was a British oversight, sir. The police just passed the information on to Carter about the two women. There was no identity check. Even I didn't know until two days later.'

The engines roared briefly and the aircraft began to pick up speed down the runway. 'And have they bought it?' Reinecke asked. 'Do you have any confirmation?' He was already unbuckling his seat belt, reaching for another Chesterfield.

With more confidence than he felt, Kagan said, 'They'll buy it, sir. It's a very refined set-up. We'll hear soon enough.'

But the inquiry had gone home, started a train of thought. Three weeks now, and they hadn't heard from Alexandrevitch. He'd missed the rendezvous with Avery in Rome four days before.

Avery had spent three hours watching a mangy camel in Rome Zoo, and an hour at the second rendezvous at the Baths of Caracalla the same evening, but there had been no sign of the Russian. It had been a nice irony for Maskelyne to suggest the Baths of Caracalla. Avery's interest in antiquities was minimal. His nearest approach to culture was a reluctant evening or two at the Theatre of Comedy.

The smoke had begun to irritate his eyes. He wondered if the senator would be offended if he moved. Reinecke was already at his papers, marking them off with a slim gold pen.

'I'm just going to stretch out on the seats over there, sir. I only had four hours last night.'

Reinecke grunted bad-temperedly. 'As much as I ever have. Suit yourself.'

Kagan lay on the two seats across the gangway from the senator and closed his eyes. His indigestion was so bad it felt as though he was having a heart attack. And he'd have to tell Reinecke about the Commission of Inquiry. Perhaps tonight, after the official reception and a few drinks. Not that Reinecke drank, he reflected mournfully. Still, he'd find a way.

At about the same time that Senator Reinecke's plane was taking off, Sir Joseph Sainsbury was sitting in Sally Kane's flat just off Curzon Street. Maskelyne had arranged the meeting, commenting over the phone with an unexpected suggestion of humour, 'She's giving up work for the afternoon in your honour.'

The flat had surprised him with its restrained good taste. There was a bookcase fronted with wooden Doric columns which boasted some unusual works: Burton's *Anatomy of Melancholy* sat next to Cicero's *On the Nature of the Gods*; Lucan, Catullus, Pliny, Livy, Herodotus. The *chaise-longue*'s subtle pinks and greens matched the swagged curtains, and the wall over the chimneybreast sported an original Atkinson Grimshaw. Joseph was leaning on his stick examining the books when an amused voice behind him said, 'Not another person who thinks it odd that whores have taste, surely?' and then, mock seriously, without pausing, 'But we know that the great and good Sir Joseph Sainsbury never makes such summary judgements, don't we?'

When they were seated a maid appeared with a salver and some coffee cups. She looked about sixteen and Joseph wondered if she was one of Sally Kane's trainees. Watching the girl leave, he was aware of Sally Kane's amused gaze. He watched her pour the coffee and reflected that loose morals often seemed to go with a liquid grace of movement. He could see why men found Sally Kane attractive. What he could not see was why she had chosen such a life, when her endowments could have given her a life as the mistress of some great house in respectable society.

As though reading his thoughts, she said, 'I expect you're wondering why I became a whore,' smiling at his discomfiture. She sat down on the chair opposite him, crossing one elegant leg over the other. She wore a simple crocheted top, and a pale pink flared skirt. Her neck and shoulders were deep honey. Her bell of hair, artfully coiffed to seem casual, was the palest blonde. Joseph suspected that she was aware of the effect her beauty was having on him, and felt uneasy again.

'In a way it was the Brig,' she said. 'Sometimes he used to call me up and invite me to make up numbers at a party. Oh, don't get me wrong. There was nothing that Julia, for all her Russian suspicions, could have accused us of.' She paused for a moment, smiling with some private amusement. 'Anyway . . . ', she leaned forward to take a biscuit from the tray, and Joseph raised his eyes to the ceiling to avoid the temptation of looking down her neckline, ' . . . I realized that I could have this life permanently if I gave up those convent schoolgirl thoughts of faithful domesticity. To tell the truth it had never appealed to me, after a few thoughts about marriage in my teens. I could never really accustom myself to the idea of being a man's possession.'

The girl came back to clear away the coffee cups. A police-car siren sounded in Piccadilly, growing louder and then fading. Joseph fumbled in his pocket for one of his pills. The pains had begun again, and he wanted his mind to be clear. It was the nights he had begun to dread since his visit to Andre. The darkness, the silence of the sleeping city, the atavistic premonition that, if consciousness remained, it would take this form. Alone in the dark forever. But Lucifer's words were right. For who would lose, though full of pain, this intellectual being, these thoughts that wander through eternity . . .

Sally Kane paused for a moment, looking at him with sympathy, and resumed. David Marsh's suicide had been tragic, she agreed, but it was hard to understand why he had felt so despairing in this day and age. After all, many politicians played around. And if it wasn't with people like her, it was with their secretaries, or with other men's wives. If women understood men's natures better, stopped making such a song and dance about something so natural and intrinsically unimportant, the world would be a simpler place. Her tone was smug, as though to suggest that she had found the secrets, that they were the product of intelligent thought, the sort of thinking that belonged with the pictures, with the stacked volumes in the bookcase.

At one stage Joseph said shyly, 'But don't you miss having children?' and she had paused. She glanced away and down for a moment, and then looked him defiantly in the eyes. 'No,' she said, and he knew that she was lying. She lied, too, when he asked her about Alexandrevitch, affecting only to remember the Russian with difficulty. But one thing worried him most of all, long after he had left the flat and was walking up New Bond Street as the late afternoon sun slanted across the tops of the buildings. Why had Sally Kane referred to Julia's 'Russian suspicions'?

Burberry took the earphones off and picked up the phone. He dialled a number, drumming his fingers on the table as he waited for a response. After a few moments he said, 'He's left now, sir. I'll put the tape on.' He switched the tape through and sat back, looking at the little fair-haired girl who was reading a comic on the dusty sofa. He glanced at his watch. At least an hour and a half before confirmation.

'Come on,' he said. 'I'll beat you at Scrabble.' Insofar as he was fond of anything he had a soft spot for children. For preference he'd have dogs, provided they didn't wreck the garden. But children were all right.

An hour later she was asleep, sucking her thumb. Burberry sat at the desk, looking down at the drab suburban street. Behind him the spool whirred through to the end.

When the reels stopped turning he picked up the receiver. He listened, nodding his head in mute acknowledgement, and then put the receiver down. It was dusk now, and the light from the lamp on the desk barely penetrated the gloom at the far end of the room. He could just make out the child's features.

After a moment he picked up the receiver again and dialled a number. He waited, stubbing out his dead cigar with displaced attention until he heard a voice at the other end. 'No call back. That was fine,' he said. 'I'm taking Belinda back to your sister in a little while.' He replaced the receiver, ignoring the caller's questions. He put the tape recorder into a canvas bag, and walked over and shook the sleeping child gently. 'Come on. Time to go,' he said. He locked the door carefully behind him and held the little girl's hand as they walked down the rickety staircase and out to the car.

11

James Bergman looked out of the window of his flat in Belsize Grove. It was six-thirty in the morning, and he could hear the distant whirr and crump of the refuse cart making its way up Haverstock Hill. He remembered how, just a few weeks ago, he would occasionally wake early and draw the curtains to watch one of the girls in the Swedish hostel opposite doing her exercises, stark naked, in front of the open window. That seemed like a lifetime ago.

Now, if he slept at all, he woke up almost invariably at around three. At first he had thought that the memories, the guilt, would fade, but they seemed to have attained a keener cutting edge in the four months since Anna's death. He had almost accepted that it must have been an appalling coincidence, but sometimes, remembering the classical quotations from his university days, he wondered at their truth: those whom the gods wish to destroy they first make mad; like flies to wanton boys are we to the gods, they kill us for their sport. He was partly aware of the self-deceiving nature of such thoughts. He knew that they gave responsibility to some superior force; that he could say if he wished, 'What could I do? It was nothing to do with me.' And, somewhere, he knew that the relief was only temporary.

It was always those early days which returned to memory first, as wakefulness returned. Lying between sleep and waking he could recapture the exact texture of those first meetings, the precise and unexpected tenderness Anna aroused in him, the later feelings of part hopelessness because the total possession his nature craved was so tenuous, of such temporary duration. A few moments of ecstasy, of oneness, when he would lie with his mouth on hers, the soft, rank smell of sweat in his nostrils, the frantic pulse of her movements beneath him. An agonizing insight into the transience of her feelings towards him had come early. He tortured himself with the memory of returning home and letting himself in quietly, planning to surprise her with a bunch of roses. She was in the bedroom in her dressing gown, her head swathed in a towel, talking on the phone. And, as he stood in the hall savouring the moment to come, she had said, 'But he doesn't know, darling . . . ', turning with a smile which stayed fixed when she saw him. 'Oh, it's you,' she said. He always remembered that.

The drinking hadn't helped. Nor had Helen, though he had found a temporary relief in her bed. It was when she said wistfully, 'We seem to fit together so well,' one morning, still in her dressing-gown, perched on the edge of the bed as they ate their toast and marmalade, that he realized the indulgence of seeking comfort from her without any long-term commitment. The night before, James had noticed Burberry sitting in a dark corner of the wine bar, and a few nights before that he had seen in the night club another man he was sure worked for the Bureau. For the first time since he had joined the Service he just didn't care.

He had escorted Lydia to David Marsh's funeral, prompted by a sense of obligation. That was a month ago. He wasn't sure whether he felt relieved or despondent that the strained intimacy of the evening he had taken her to her sister's seemed to have vanished without trace. She had said something before they left, standing in the porch for a moment to recover from sudden grief. 'The coroner was wrong. David just wasn't the type to commit suicide.'

He'd looked at her face under the veil, the startling blue eyes staring into space. Before he could respond the two boys had come down the stairs with Mrs Baines, and it was time to go. Only David's PPS and the Atkins had been there to represent the government. There were a few personal friends, and, of course, the photographers, angling to get their shots of the widow throwing earth on the coffin. He'd tried to protect her from that, feeling a bond of sympathy with her through a sense of common loss. Not that he could tell her about Anna. Not now, perhaps not ever. Avery had done his job so well that none of the papers had even printed their names. 'Two women from Greenham Common in death mystery at Porton Down' had been the nearest any of the dailies had come to it. He had not seen Anna go into the earth, and the sense of incompleteness, almost the feeling that she was not dead, had remained. Marsh's funeral had given him a strange opportunity to vent his grief. By the graveside the tears ran down his face, and he was half aware of Lydia's curiosity. He had taken her out to lunch since then, and had gone with her and the boys for a picnic on Box Hill a week later. Though they talked of other things, with a conventional distance between them, there was a mutuality in their sorrow, bringing them closer together.

Three days ago he had received an unexpected caller at the flat. Carter ('Crater' or 'the Black Hole' to his friends and enemies alike), Kagan's assistant. One of the lean, crew-cut, anonymous young men with dead eyes. He had ventured trivia at first, walking restlessly around the flat as though taking an inventory, a glass of bourbon in his hand. The weather. Baseball. James had silently carried on with preparing his dinner, knowing that the questions would become more pointed. He walked into the kitchen to put the take-away into the oven. Carter followed him, leaning against the door frame, waving his hand against the offer of a share. 'I've eaten already.' He watched James setting the tray in silence.

It will come now, James thought, with all the reflexes built into him by the department. He took the oven gloves out of the top drawer, putting them on top of the hob in readiness.

'The boss is a little worried about you,' Carter ventured. The Harvard certainty in his voice had been replaced by a softer, less definite cadence. James said nothing, laying the tray with meticulous neatness. A white paper napkin, a knife, a fork, a spoon, a perspex cruet.

Carter shifted position against the door frame.

'Frankly,' he said, 'we need you back on station, fully operational. We've made three efforts to contact Alexandrevitch without success. Two weeks to go before the talks and we don't know if it's worked or not . . . ' He laughed unconvincingly. 'We need someone to go in, full tourist identity, to see what's going on.'

James felt furiously angry, suddenly. After what had happened, how dare they ask him? Anyway, his card was profiled 'Not suitable for Eastern Europe'. For Christ's sake, they must know it would be impossible after his open tour with Maskelyne.

'No dice, Charlie,' he said, controlling his voice as much as possible. 'With my profile I'd be in Lubianka in a day, being worked over by Grishkin or Kalevsky himself.' He couldn't keep the bitterness from his voice. 'Not that I could tell them very much. Or does Kagan think I'm expendable too?'

Carter sounded shocked. 'He talks about you like a son, Jimmy. You know that.' He paused for a moment and said carefully, 'Actually it was my idea. We haven't really discussed it . . . '

Carter's arm slipped on the door jamb, and his coat flapped open, exposing the shoulder holster for a moment. 'You know how important this job is . . .'

Bergman turned to face the taller man. He wondered wildly for an instant if he could reach Carter, scythe an arm across his neck, before the other man reached his gun. Careful, he said to himself, it's not his fault. He's only part of the system. He spoke as deliberately as possible, measuring his words.

'No, Charlie. That's just it. I don't know what was important enough to set me up to kill my own wife. I don't know what was important enough to call for the death of David Marsh. I don't know what is important enough to send me to almost certain imprisonment in Lubianka. Tell me, Charlie. Is it an order?'

Carter leaned forward and put his glass down on the unit top. 'I told you we hadn't discussed it. It's not an order. Merely a suggestion. Kagan thought you might welcome some action to take you out of yourself.' He turned to go, buttoning the middle button of his jacket. 'Think it over, James. I've thought of the angles. Kalevsky wouldn't anticipate a member of the department coming over on business.'

James closed the door behind Carter. He was angry with himself for perspiring, for feeling shaky with rage. After a few moments he walked over to the large window in the sitting-room which overlooked Belsize Grove. Carter was walking towards his BMW. He looked up and smiled, waving his hand. James stepped back into the room. He wondered what to believe, now. The cell system cut across everything, made everything uncertain. Perhaps Carter was telling the truth. Perhaps it wasn't Kagan's idea. Perhaps.

He felt better after calling Lydia. Yes, she'd be delighted to come to dinner tomorrow evening. Her voice sounded warm. For the first time in months he felt, to his surprise, a sense of pleasurable anticipation. At least Kagan hadn't said anything about his seeing Lydia, yet. Not that he would have paid any attention. He felt alienated from the department, from his past work. He ate his supper off the tray on his knees, looking out at the darkening street. What other sort of work was he fit for, he wondered. It was hard to think of working in an office, leaving on the same train every day, waiting for promotion, the salary increase, the rise in London Weighting Allowance. He recognized in himself a small contempt for people who worked in offices for limited ends. And, at the back of his mind, Lydia's convinced statement about her husband before the funeral teased at his mind.

'David just wasn't the type to commit suicide.'

12

Joseph Sainsbury sat in the brown leather armchair in front of his desk, looking out over Fitzroy Square. It was three days since his visit to Sally Kane, and seven hours since Honecker had returned his call over the terrible line from Warsaw.

He poured himself a glass of whisky from the ship's decanter on his desk. He had called Andre earlier to cancel the bridge evening at the club. 'No. No. I'm fine, really,' he had protested in response to his friend's anxious inquiries. 'I just feel like an evening on my own.' Now he sat and thought about David Marsh, Sally Kane, Pyotr Alexandrevitch and, above all, about the contents of Fritz Honecker's telephone call.

Honecker owed him a debt of gratitude from the war. On the few occasions Joseph had seen him since then, mainly when they met on international charity commissions to which Joseph was an adviser, Honecker had never failed to ask how he could repay his debt. He had done so now, with interest and, Joseph suspected, with some risk to himself. Joseph had not asked him how he had got this information. He knew it could not have been easy. He took a sheet of paper from the red folder on his desk, and re-read what he had written. Below the four entries already there he began to write in his neat, cursive hand:

Ludmilla Terreshkova: b. 15.4.31.
Warsaw University 49/52, Dept. Mech. Sci.
Hons. Degree 52.
53/59 Superviser Mech. Eng. Spolenta Technik Fabricca.
59. Daughter Olga. Birth certificate registers 'Father unknown'.
No further information.
File marked 'Closed'.

Honecker suggests this may mean defection to W. Germany based upon other files.

He stopped writing and looked out of the window. On a ledge across the other side of the square a row of pigeons sat, ruffling their feathers and tucking their heads under their wings. The leaves danced on the trees. In sudden fear, he felt his death waiting in the shadows. How long, he wondered. Please God, not before he had finished this, his last task.

He took a sip of whisky, put his glass down meticulously on the cork coaster and picked up his pen again. He wrote the figure six in the margin, and against it:

Sally Kane/child? Not reliable.

After a moment he wrote a seven in the margin. He put the heading 'To be questioned' and underlined it twice, and then wrote down some names:

James Bergman
Lydia Marsh
(Kagan)?
(Maskelyne)?

He gazed out of the window for a long time. Some aspects of what was happening here worried him. He thought back to the Profumo case. After all, he thought, what real improprieties were committed there beyond ordinary, human failings? Lying to the House – well, everyone did that in some degree or other. The parallel with Ivanov and the possible breach of security? There seemed to Joseph some tremendous psychological absurdity in the notion that men bent upon illicit sexual pleasure would spill out vital defence secrets to high-class whores, or to Russian military attachés. Burgess, Maclean, Philby, Vassall, Blunt – all these had been different. And, Joseph thought, it is a peculiar hypocrisy of the English that we behave as though our hands were clean in this, as though we didn't have our sources in the Warsaw Pact countries.

It still astonished him, a quarter of a century later, to remember the ripples caused by Christine Keeler and Mandy Rice-Davies. True, there had been peripheral information the suppression of which had possibly contributed to the sense of deceit, of guarded secrets. The alleged close association between Stephen Ward and certain members of the Royal Family. He began to realize that what was worrying him now, as it had then, was the question of what the Establishment was trying to hide. He had no wish now, nor ever had, to be used as a tool of that Establishment, however nobly the Brigadier might dress up the cause. Nor had he any belief in the morality of Maskelyne's grey masters. Cynically he thought that, to them as to the politicians, truth was whatever happened to be convenient at the appropriate time. He sighed, refilling his glass. He had never subscribed to that belief, and now less than ever, with the features of his death grinning nightly ever nearer over his shoulder.

It was past midnight when he went to bed. He did now what he had never done before, half ashamed at the theatricality of his own thoughts. He secured the windows with the burglar-proof locks; he opened the door and looked out on to the peaceful landing, then closed it again and shot the bolt home at the top, securing the chain. He had never before noticed the sounds of night: the gurgling of the central heating system, the creaking of the chairs as the temperature slowly dropped, the motor humming as the fridge turned on.

Ashamed of his fears, he got undressed and into his pyjamas, and lay reading Gibbon's *Decline and Fall* until the early hours, propped among his pillows like a vast, socialized bear.

13

Pyotr Alexandrevitch had followed Grishkin's instructions to the letter. He felt alone, neither able to keep his appointment in Rome with Avery nor to shake Viktor off so that he could cue into the alternative message service in Yuri's flat. He suspected, anyway, that there would be no contingency plans. The only slim comfort he had was that his masters in Whitehall and Washington would need some confirmation of the success (or otherwise) of their strategy. Not that he could give them anything beyond his own interpretation. Since the meeting with Grishkin he had heard nothing further. Only the constant presence of Viktor reminded him that, somewhere in the grey recesses of the KGB offices, his fate and such information as he had given Grishkin must be under review.

He had even bought Viktor a couple of drinks and engaged him in innocuous conversations. The tourist trade, Russia's success in space, the Chernobyl disaster. The other man's responses, so depressingly predictable, had reminded him afresh of the reasons for his own defection. That his countrymen should accept such obvious falsehoods diminished them in his eyes. After a while he took to avoiding the tourist bar at the Sputnik. Not that it made any difference. Wherever he went, Viktor, or one of his two replacements, was always there, the regulation twenty yards behind.

He had continued, dutifully, to act like a tourist. At the Panorama Museum of the Battle of Borodino he had stood for fifteen minutes in front of Franz Rubo's painting depicting an episode between the Russian army and Napoleon's troops. At the Central Lenin Museum he had affected great interest in Lenin's manuscripts and memorabilia, deriving some pleasure from Viktor's evident boredom. He had even forced himself to visit the Pushkin Fine Arts Museum. It was difficult to know what was worse: the seemingly interminable boredom or the loneliness. He had never before realized to what extent his life relied upon parties, upon other people, upon the ordinary excitements and exchanges of daily living in contact with friends. He hadn't dared to pick up a woman, as was his habit on less onerous assignments, and the fear which had become so insistent and ever present had dampened his customary sexual urges.

The evenings were the worst. He had endured a terrible evening at the Maly – a turgid performance of *The Cherry Orchard* which had sent him to sleep until the closing applause woke him. (It hadn't been like that when he was twenty-five, holding Irina's hand while they listened to the Beryozka Ensemble: but that had been another life.) He found, too, that his old ability to relish the excitement of fear and insecurity which were so much part of his life had deserted him. He would lie on his bed, sleepless, for half the night, wondering what Kalevsky might have in store for him. The mere thought of Kalevsky made him feel sick, so that he would sometimes stand over the basin retching spasmodically. He had met Kalevsky once in the old days, when Beria ran things. There had been nothing frightening about the man's appearance: short, swarthy, with the suspicious manner of a small-towner slightly in awe of Muscovite society. But he knew, too, that Grishkin was only a pale imitation of his master. Kalevsky had been an Andropov appointee and, however he may have seemed as a young major when Pyotr first met him, he was now, by reputation at least, the most sophisticated of Muscovites. Despite his inveterate womanizing and prodigious capacity for vodka he had survived the purge that followed Gorbachev's accession to the post of General Secretary. Perhaps, Pyotr thought, lying on his bed and drinking his vodka, Kalevsky couldn't be removed because he knew too much. Like J. Edgar Hoover. The little joke didn't serve to cheer him up.

When it happened it was completely unexpected. He'd spent the early afternoon at the Andrei Rublev Museum of Early Russian Art. To alleviate his boredom he had tagged on to the end of an American tourist party, all giving their earnest attention and much vocal appreciation to their guide, a young Russian in his thirties who spoke the execrable English of Intourist guides. He decided to go back to the hotel and brew a cup of tea, almost convinced by now that he would never hear further – from anyone. As he entered the room he saw Viktor by the window, and the place in complete disarray. A moment later he felt a crushing blow to his head, and felt his nose break as he fell face down on the floor. The salty taste of blood in his mouth reminded him of fighting as a schoolboy. Then nothing.

It must have been around eight hours later when he awoke. He was in a cell barely eight feet by four, with a grille window high in the wall opposite the door. He was lying on a pallet, naked except for his Marks and Spencer underpants. They had taken his watch, too, and he surmised it must be late because the window showed no light. He took stock of his surroundings by the feeble glow from the forty-watt bulb hanging from the ceiling, high above his reach. His head ached abominably.

The smell in the cell was terrible. He could just see, from the traces of excrement in the corner and the fetid smell, that the previous occupant had also been denied toilet facilities. He advanced gingerly towards the corner and urinated. He realized that he was hungry, and debated whether or not he should call out. Better not, he thought, reluctant to call anyone who might decide to hit him about the head again. He sat down to wait. Once there was a noise at the door, and he saw the small shutter move aside and an impersonal eye appear. It looked briefly at him, and slowly surveyed the rest of the cell. Then it closed again, and he was left alone with his thoughts. He suspected that he was in some part of the KGB buildings. There were none of the prison noises he remembered from his visits to Gyorgy Arbatov, who was serving a life sentence for the killing of his wife: the boots echoing down concrete corridors, the rattle of keys, the guttural cross-chat of the warders. There was only an eerie silence.

He lost track of time. As the ache in his head lessened he found that his front teeth hurt, were loose, and that his nose really was broken. This is a fine mess you've landed yourself in this time, Pyotr Alexandrevitch, he said, trying to joke the fear away, without success. Just as he was beginning to fall into an uneasy sleep the door opened, and an arm pushed a tin tray gratingly across the floor. The door clanged shut again, instantly.

Black bread and thin tea. Despite the pain of eating he attacked the bread, tearing it into small pieces so that he could chew it comfortably. The tea was grey and tasteless, but it helped to wash down the dry, stale bread.

He fell asleep. The sound of the door opening awoke him and he rolled over to find a very bright light shining in his eyes. There were two figures behind the light, but it was too bright for him to make anything out beyond the vague outlines of a tall man and a stocky, smaller one. He could not even make out which of them spoke.

'Pyotr Alexandrevitch. We have reason to think you are in the pay of anti-Soviet agents. What have you to say?'

He felt a strange relief. So they were going to try those hoary old tricks, thinking that if they terrified him enough he would tell all he knew. It was standard procedure, even when they were interrogating someone whose credentials as a lover of the Motherland appeared impeccable.

'Comrade,' Pyotr said, 'you only have to ask the President, who is an old friend. Such a statement is ridiculous.'

The other voice was softer, more persuasive. 'All we have heard from Comrade Grishkin is vague and unsubstantiated rumour. As you know, these talks are almost upon us. We need more. Tell us . . .'

Ah well, Pyotr thought. It's time for the set speech. The light hurt his eyes and he closed them, feeling suddenly ridiculous, semi-naked in front of this bright light.

'It was easier in the old days,' he said. 'Powers, the others, would just go up in a plane and take back photographs for analysis. But later our missiles were detected in Cuba by Kennedy's planes without any difficulty . . .' He was aware that he was losing their interest and pressed on, suddenly afraid of the possibility of violence. 'The British had always felt they were junior partners in their relations with America. You will remember there was trouble about Cruise in Britain, about how the decisions for use would be taken. Joint control or . . . the special relationship . . .' He had their attention now. Suddenly conscious of his hands, he put them behind his back. 'Just after the Falklands War patriotism, the sense of national identity, pride, ran very high in Britain. It was decided then to take steps which would re-establish them as a major political and military power. And this time they wouldn't pass the information across for others to make use of. After all, since de Gaulle the French had pursued an independent line in testing while maintaining their place in NATO and their relationship with America . . .'

He paused, and the softer voice said, 'Go on . . .' He

couldn't tell from the tone whether the speaker was interested. But at least they were listening.

He cleared his throat and ran his tongue over dry lips.

'There was no point in their trying to participate in the hardware competition, or SDI. Firstly, these would be too expensive to legislate through Parliament. Secondly, such activities might affect their so-called special relationship. Thirdly, any developments in these areas would be too visible to the Warsaw Pact countries. So they decided to follow another path . . . '

Suddenly the spotlight was pointed towards the floor. He almost cried with relief, watching the bright retinal afterimage fade. Their faces were still invisible.

He felt more confident now. He was almost sure he would soon be back at the hotel, enjoying a vodka and a warm bath. He had never thought he would miss the hotel. He resumed.

'As you will know, there are a number of secret biological research stations in Britain. From time to time there have been queries and feature articles in the papers or in the media about them, but the British Establishment are very good at defusing such issues. They say everything is all right, show incredulity that anyone could possibly be concerned, and the public are reassured . . . '

The taller man coughed, and Pyotr thought, I'd better not make too much of a meal of it. Mustn't lose the point for the padding.

'Anyway. The Government Scientific Advisers got together in late '82. There was a Professor Butterfield working on genetic mutations at the Cavendish, and he was invited to join the first meeting.' In parentheses he added, straining to see beyond the light, 'David Marsh told me this one evening. He was very drunk, very angry. Said it cut across all the rules of civilized behaviour, all the protocols and conventions agreed to make the world a safer place . . . '

He suddenly felt the need to urinate. He said abjectly, 'Please, Comrades, may I relieve myself? It was the tea.' And, not waiting for a reply, went over to the corner. He felt humiliated, with the spotlight shining on his bare legs, and the sound of his urine splashing on the concrete floor. A trickle ran on to his foot and he stepped back with an involuntary exclamation of disgust. There was a brief laugh from one of the figures.

Where was he? Oh yes.

'I am not a scientist, Comrades,' he said, trying to infuse his voice with moral indignation about what he was about to divulge. 'But what they planned was monstrous. Professor Butterfield's task was to devise a virus – that's what I think they call it – which would produce and accelerate cancer in both humans and livestock, and which would work in such a way as to become part of the genetic inheritance of any progeny born after the incident – that is to say, the infecting of one or other parent . . . '

The harsher voice said, 'And how would delivery be made?'

'Any number of ways. By conventional warhead, via waterways, through infected supplies of certain foodstuffs sold at discount to the Soviet Union. There have been thirty top scientists and technicians working on this for over five years now . . . '

The smaller man stepped into the light. It was Kalevsky. He wore a Stalin jacket and his face still seemed that of a brutal peasant. Thank God I didn't know before, Pyotr thought fervently. Affecting not to recognize the other man, he said, 'Do you mind if I sit down, Comrade? I haven't eaten too well today.' He sat down on the edge of the wooden bunk.

Without inflection, Kalevsky said, 'But the Americans would never permit such a thing . . . '

'The Americans don't know for sure. The activities of Porton Down do not fall within their sphere of influence or their area of interest. So far as anyone not party to the conclusions of that committee are concerned, Porton Down is merely a research establishment carrying out bona fide medical and biological research. Nothing more . . . '

'So,' Kalevsky said slowly, 'the implications for the talks are that we may now have to consider the British position separately?'

This was the difficult part. Pyotr felt his hands sweat, but dared venture no movement which might indicate what he was feeling. Kalevsky had no need of lie detectors. He had seen into too many human hearts without their help.

He shifted from one foot to the other and looked down, trying to convey by his demeanour that he was putting forward the only tenable position.

'No, sir. The American forward line in Europe is now too deeply entrenched to alter it. Bringing these facts to the attention of the negotiating team would probably, in the long run, only increase American influence over their own warheads in Europe. I think that the only worthwhile deal is to offer some reduction in exchange for inspection of all facilities – including research establishments . . . ' He held his breath.

Kalevsky said abruptly, 'You're not a politician, Pyotr Alexandrevitch. These policies are not for you and me to dictate.' But Pyotr sensed that something in the other man had changed, that he had assimilated the suggestion. He relaxed slightly.

'By the way,' Kalevsky said casually, 'the two girls. One was Maskelyne's daughter, wasn't she?'

Thank God, Pyotr thought. He'd never believed in the Deity, but this deserved something. The plan had worked.

'Yes,' he said, steeling himself to sound neutral.

The voice sounded tired now. 'One last question. Why did you not give this information to my deputy when he came to visit you at the hotel?'

Pyotr lied. 'I was uncertain of his position. I knew this information must only be given to the highest authority.'

He only realized what Kalevsky was doing when the action was almost complete.

'Niet. Niet!' he shouted, his cry bouncing back from the walls. Kalevsky raised his hand with the gun in it and shot Pyotr once through the right eye. He put the gun away and looked down at Pyotr's body for a moment. 'I am the highest authority,' he said, and walked down the corridor without a backward glance. The other man put out the light and dragged the body outside the door.

Presently two men came down with a stretcher covered in a grey blanket. The younger man laughed and whispered to the other as they manoeuvred the body on to the stretcher. The older man shot him a warning glance, looking after the retreating figures. They carried the body down the long corridor in silence.

14

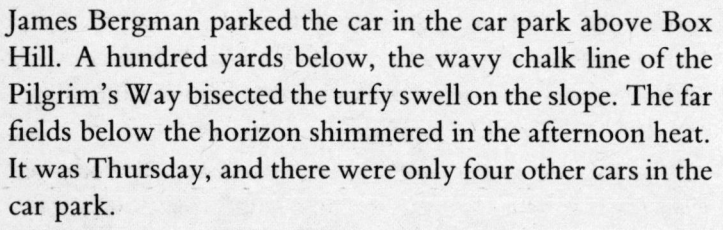

James Bergman parked the car in the car park above Box Hill. A hundred yards below, the wavy chalk line of the Pilgrim's Way bisected the turfy swell on the slope. The far fields below the horizon shimmered in the afternoon heat. It was Thursday, and there were only four other cars in the car park.

He got out quickly and opened the passenger door for Lydia. I'm becoming quite the little gentleman, he thought to himself cynically. He took her by the elbow to help her out of the car. The boys were away at school, and Lydia had surprised him by phoning to suggest this picnic a couple of days before. Despite Carter's attempt to bring him back into active operation he had continued his leave; and so far nobody had complained. He felt a strange, uncharacteristic irresponsibility, composed partly of a massive anger and loss of belief in the department, and partly of a sudden and complete crisis of faith in the tenets by which he had lived his life for so long.

He had been involved, directly and indirectly, in the death of others often before. Somehow it had always seemed merely an accident, set against the wider causes which seemed to justify the expedience of the killing. 'Termination with extreme prejudice' was the phrase which had somehow crept into common parlance in America. It had been one of the Bureau's ways of distancing such events. Often it had been a Rivers or an Avery who had performed the actual deed, and he had found that this company, and this licence to commit murder without any fear of the law, had conferred a certain godlike power.

Sometimes circumstances had forced his hand. Once he had killed with a knife in Poznan, and once with a gun when he was training with the police in New York. ('Waste him. Waste him!' the sergeant had yelled, and he had pulled the trigger and felt nothing.) There had been a curious numbness in the doing of these things, and he had slept easily afterwards. Now, because it had been Anna, and again because of this growing, painful intimacy with Lydia, he felt himself experiencing an almost religious insight into the complications of killing another human being. Unused to introspection (it was actively discouraged by the Bureau), he had been surprised by his own reactions to Anna's death: the thoughts and feelings which had visited him unbidden in the months following had sprung from some deep well within him, irrepressible, and worrying in its effect upon his usually controlled and ordered life.

He took the hamper out of the car and locked the door. At the road end of the long car park he saw Carter's BMW nose into the entrance. He waved facetiously and Lydia said, 'Who's that?', wrinkling her eyes against the sun. 'Oh, just an acquaintance,' he said, smiling down at her. She had an openness in her eyes now, a vulnerability which reminded him of Anna when they first met. She stumbled against a tussock, holding out her hand to steady herself, and he saw the swell of her breast through the open neckline of her cerise blouse.

'Hey, steady now,' he said, feeling an excitement he had not felt for years. Walking down the slope she caught hold of his hand unselfconsciously, and again he had that brief sensation of hope and anticipation which he had never thought to feel again. Walking down the hill they talked about trivia, as though to discount the implication of their joined hands. Two couples walked diagonally up the hill across their path, accompanied by a joyous, barking collie which scurried to and fro, herding an imaginary flock of sheep. Once James looked back over his shoulder to see Carter, immaculate in green tweeds and a deerstalker, slowly picking his way down after them. He seemed out of place. He had always been a corridors-of-power man rather than the rougher end of the trade.

'What about here?' Lydia gestured towards a patch of shade under a hawthorn. A bramble thicket enclosed it on three sides, shielding them from the majority of walkers. Even Carter was no longer in sight. Red berries hung in the luminous green shade of the bush.

No, he wasn't to do anything, she ordered with surprising firmness. He was amused. He had noticed in her a tendency he found endearingly old-fashioned: the habit of seeing certain jobs as 'women's work'. He lay back on his elbow, watching her unpack the hamper. She talked about her childhood: the convent school in Kent, the old house with its huge rooms, its air of history and permanence. Of her father, whose inheritance had left him free to potter through life and indulge his obsessive love of gardening; of her mother, and her mother's admirers, about whom Lydia and her sister had speculated endlessly as children. 'Poor thing,' Lydia said, unwrapping the salad container from its clingfilm with careful fingers, 'she didn't really get very much from father.' As she talked James had a vision of a golden childhood, secure, peopled with loving relatives and faithful retainers, and imbued with that perception of childhood: that life and happiness will carry on for ever. Almost he felt envy, contrasting, as she spoke, his own impoverished parents on the family smallholding. The winds whistling pitilessly, the lean livestock with fly-encrusted eyes rooting through the brown dust for the sere grass. And, with the near envy he felt, came also the desire for possession. It had been the same with Anna. The aphrodisiac had been a combination of her and, importantly, of that heritage of old houses, heirloom silver, history; above all, of that childhood which she, too, had talked about with such careless indifference. That was in her, and had made her, as it had been in Anna in those first rapturous days before the darkness began.

The wind occasionally rose, momentarily stealing the heat from the sun. Far above them a skylark stuttered in erratic flight, throwing its desperate song into the air. Around them the bees flew clumsily from blossom to blossom. James ate lazily, almost happy for the first time in months. There was no past, no tomorrow, as things had been in childhood. Lydia said, 'A penny for them,' taking her hair back with a gesture of her white arm, and he looked at her uncomprehendingly. 'For your thoughts, I mean,' she said, laughing. 'They're not worth that,' he said, and then, 'much more. I was thinking of you.' Under the olive skin of her cheek he saw the colour rise, and she looked down at her plate and they were silent for a time.

When they had eaten he folded the cloth carefully and put it in the hamper. Then the plates and glasses, first brushing the plates free from crumbs and wiping the glasses with a tissue. 'So neat,' said Lydia, her eyes resting on him speculatively. 'Did your wife teach you?' And he knew that she was really asking other things about Anna which were much more important. (Not yet the things he knew she really wanted to hear about, but closer.) So he told her some of it. Not about the Brigadier being her father, or about the manner of her death. But about most other things. She watched him with sympathetic eyes, nodding to show her understanding of a phrase or a nuance in his expression. When he looked away from her and said, 'She's dead,' his voice carried such a bitter inflection that she wanted to comfort him. She put out her hand to touch his shoulder, and then was in his arms. He felt the heat of her body through his thin shirt, and her lips open beneath his, the smell of her warm hair in his nostrils. This is now, different, he thought fiercely, trying to banish those early memories of Anna from his mind. She moved so that her leg was under his, her breath quickening in his ear, and he rolled so that he now lay on top of her.

On the slope above him he caught a movement in a gap in the brambles. Ludicrously, it seemed for a moment that the bush had sprouted a head, together with a deerstalker. Carter's sunglasses hid his eyes as he looked down at them. Before James could move, the head had disappeared. His desire had gone as suddenly as it had come. 'What's the matter?' Lydia asked, her lips moving against his shoulder, and he stroked her cheek gently. 'We're too old for this country romancing,' he said awkwardly, pulling her to her feet. 'Come and see where I live.'

During the long journey to Belsize Park they were stilted, selfconscious with each other. James cursed Carter in his mind, but automatically, without heat, knowing that the other man was only following instructions. The awkwardness continued when they got to the flat and, for the first time, James was suddenly aware of the bare masculinity of the place. 'Would you like a drink?' he asked, but she walked towards him and took the bottle of whisky from his hand and put it on the sideboard. She put her arms around his neck and stood on the ball of her right foot, wrapping the other leg round his upper thigh, so that he was almost caught off balance. He was surprised by the passion in her movements. 'Oh, please. Please,' she said, kissing him with small kisses down his neck. He felt strangely breathless, moving tentatively to undo her blouse, but she moved more quickly, undoing the buttons of his shirt and covering his chest with small animal nuzzlings and bites. He undid her blouse and she slipped out of it, moving her hands behind her back to open the clip of her brassiere. Her breasts were golden, with the slight marks of stretching from childbearing running towards the nipples. He bent to kiss her left breast and she began to move her pelvis against him with strong, urgent movements. He laid her on the bed and took off her skirt and knickers, she watching his face all the while with wide eyes, and her lips half parted. She lay with her slim legs apart, in an attitude of abandonment which, slightly shocking him, yet hardened his desire. He could see the moist lips of her sex gleaming pinkly in the honey hair.

He undressed quickly, his movements clumsied by desire. He kissed her hard and moved his hand to the inside of her thigh, but she held his wrist and said, 'Come inside me now. Please. Please,' and he entered her. They moved together as one person, rocking against the hard springing of the bed. Her eyes were glazed, and he felt the movement of her hips quicken and take on an urgent rhythm of their own. 'Oh, my God,' she said, almost exultantly, 'oh, my God,' and he felt the rippling begin within her as his own orgasm started. Afterwards they lay silent awhile, her limp body resting in the crook of his arm. He turned to look at her face, calm now and covered with small beads of moisture, and felt a turning tenderness in his heart. There was gratitude, and fear, too, of what might now be beginning. There was so much yet unsaid which could alter the future, might make her turn from him in disgust. He felt an insane desire to confess everything, to say to her, 'That is all of it' – so that they could begin without shadows, without reservation. But that was impossible, and he knew somewhere, in that instant, that there could be no future in this.

And Lydia. Laughing inside at first with happiness, and with the relief of being desired, being possessed, she then began to wonder at what she had done. She knew that the remorse was there, the small voice which would castigate her for her sin in the night, the picture of Sister Mary's serene face framed by the wimple telling her that she had sinned and must repent. But for now this was enough, whatever was to come.

After a little while James got up and walked to the window. Through the net curtain he could see Carter's car and, through the windscreen, Carter's hands holding a newspaper on the wheel. He turned back towards Lydia. She was resting on her elbow, with one knee raised unselfconsciously. She surprised him by saying, 'Is he there?' and James said stupidly, 'Who?', temporarily thrown by the question. 'The man who followed us this morning,' she said, 'the one who spies on me.'

He affected not to understand. She said, with a strange intensity, 'I've been followed since David's death. I think they want to know what was in the letter he left for me in the study. I've put it away in the safe.' Don't tell me any more, he thought, sitting on the bed and putting an arm round her shoulder. Her skin was cold now. As though talking to a child, he said, very carefully and clearly, 'Lydia. You must give the letter to your solicitor or your bank manager for safe keeping. It might be dangerous to keep it at home.'

'It wasn't the letter of a man who intended to commit suicide,' she said. 'I thought of producing it at the inquest, but you know how coroners can twist things. It's true it was a confession of his . . . ' she searched for a moment for the right word, ' . . . affair with that woman, but it was an affirmation of our love for each other, too.' Tears slid down her face, and she wiped them away with a corner of the sheet. 'I realized that anybody who didn't know him as I did wouldn't know that. I realized that to anyone else it could look like a last letter.'

James's voice sounded strange in his own ears. 'You haven't shown it to anyone?' he asked, and she shook her head. 'Brigadier Maskelyne asked to see it, but he didn't press. He was so kind,' she said, her voice breaking.

He felt sick, indecisive. There seemed nowhere to take her where she would be safe. He felt that he couldn't tell her any more, prevented by some old perceptions of those early days of indoctrination: love of country, honour, patriotism. When he put his arm around her now he felt passionless, drained, and the excitement of a few moments before had gone.

He began to dress. 'Give the letter to your solicitor,' he said without expression. She looked at him for a moment with puzzlement, then averted her face and began to dress. Neither of them spoke until they were on their way, and in the car their conversation was desultory and awkward. Nor did either of them comment on the car that had nosed out behind them, and followed them at a discreet distance all the way back to Lydia's house.

15

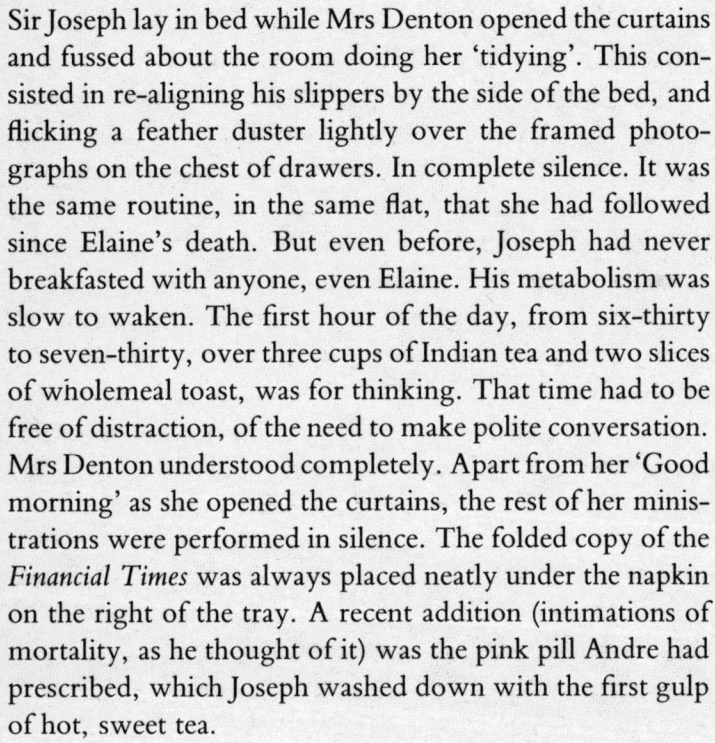

Sir Joseph lay in bed while Mrs Denton opened the curtains and fussed about the room doing her 'tidying'. This consisted in re-aligning his slippers by the side of the bed, and flicking a feather duster lightly over the framed photographs on the chest of drawers. In complete silence. It was the same routine, in the same flat, that she had followed since Elaine's death. But even before, Joseph had never breakfasted with anyone, even Elaine. His metabolism was slow to waken. The first hour of the day, from six-thirty to seven-thirty, over three cups of Indian tea and two slices of wholemeal toast, was for thinking. That time had to be free of distraction, of the need to make polite conversation. Mrs Denton understood completely. Apart from her 'Good morning' as she opened the curtains, the rest of her ministrations were performed in silence. The folded copy of the *Financial Times* was always placed neatly under the napkin on the right of the tray. A recent addition (intimations of mortality, as he thought of it) was the pink pill Andre had prescribed, which Joseph washed down with the first gulp of hot, sweet tea.

Before he began his breakfast he always looked round the room, savouring its familiarity. It was full of dim memories of Russia, from where his parents had come as refugees when he was a child. The silver-framed sepia photographs of shaggily bearded men in outlandish robes clutching rifles. The samovar which sat on the mantel. The Byzantine triptych which hung on the chimneybreast, with its doleful Madonna holding an improbably long-legged infant Jesus. The rugs, threadbare and old, which covered the floor. Now, more than ever before, he felt a poignancy in this daily ritual, aware that the sands of his life were running out. It had become more difficult to control the fear. Not of pain, nor of loneliness; he had suffered those enough to contemplate them without anguish. Of the annihilation of consciousness. At bridge, three nights before, he had felt a sudden urge to plead with Andre, as though he were a child and Andre possessed those magical powers which young children perceive in their parents: as though Andre could save him from illness, and hurt, and death.

It was better today. The sun streamed through the windows, setting the dancing motes of dust alight. As usual, he had formulated his plans for the day earlier in the week, and Mrs Plunkett (restored to her normal state) had made all the arrangements with her customary dry efficiency. He was due to pick up Lydia Marsh from her house at twelve sharp and take her for lunch in Buckingham. She was, in a sense, one of the least important interviewees on his list. He had reflected that the old cliché was true: the spouse was usually the last to know about matters of importance. But it was always his habit to leave nothing unexamined, and to approach what he instinctively saw as being the central issue gradually, without preconceptions. Even given the distortions put forward by those whose insights had long since warped under the pressures of intimacy, there was often a phrase, or a comment, unimportant to the relator which held some vital key. And, at worst, it could be a pleasant diversion with a very pretty woman.

He showered and dressed with care, choosing a pale grey

pinstripe suit. Looking in the mirror to brush his hair, he surveyed his face dispassionately. He remembered a party at Balliol in his youth where he had overheard a beautiful girl say to her escort in a careless whisper, 'A brilliant mind, but so ugly,' and he had accepted her verdict as chiming with something he had always known. Age and bibulousness had not dealt kindly with him, he knew. Liver spots covered the pouches which passed for cheeks, bracketing the pugnacious mouth. The nose was a bulbous thrust of flesh. Only the eyes had something: the soft kindness of a spaniel, and something else. A shrewdness, an ability to go on looking well after the conventions of politeness and social exchange dictated they should look away.

He had read the notes on Marsh the previous night. The newspaper clippings gave little away. But it was an old habit, like reading through his notes for the following day and sleeping on them. For him, there was none of this last-minute cramming which gave false perspectives, obtruded irrelevant data. Reading the file it had been hard to think of the man as a conduit for secrets to the other side. Certainly, there was nothing of the Burgess or Blunt about him. But however summary and inaccurate such a judgement might prove, he seemed to Joseph to have possessed that inner core of strength and certainty, that outgoing nature, which accorded ill with Joseph's concept of a spy. But, again, he must not jump to conclusions. Evidence was what he required.

Over the previous weeks he had made some progress, but not a great deal. His researches at Somerset House to track down something on Sally Kane had met with little success, though the post might produce something in the future. Both Kagan and Maskelyne had been infuriatingly casual about the Russian, Alexandrevitch, and his protracted absence. 'Oh, you mean the Russki,' Kagan had said, when Joseph finally managed to get him on the phone. 'I guess he's found himself some little sloe-eyed Tartar and they're sunning themselves on the Black Sea at the moment. Anyway, what would he know?' Maskelyne, less colourfully, had said more or less the same thing but with uncharacteristic vagueness, ending with a plainly unconvincing, 'We'll see what we can do.' It didn't seem to be any deliberate attempt at obfuscation, rather that they both gave every appearance of being totally uninterested in the Russian. And the scant file he had managed to compile on Alexandrevitch told him very little.

The car came for him at ten-thirty. As they waited patiently in a traffic jam down the Marylebone Road, he found himself thinking uncharitably that he used to enjoy London more when it wasn't quite so full of tourists of every hue and disposition and, so thinking, he began to laugh, reflecting that he could hardly consider himself to be a native of his adoptive country. Hastings, his chauffeur, who had been with him for fifteen years, smiled to himself, nodding his satisfaction. He had not heard his employer laugh for a long time and, like Sir Joseph's other employees, held Joseph in great affection. As well as his generosity and fairness, he treated each of them as his equal, discussed things with them, invited their opinions.

Heading out on the A40 past the White City, Joseph glanced at his watch and Hastings, noting the gesture in the mirror, put his foot down. The traffic was thinner now, though there were still the middle-lane merchants doing forty-five, the lorries moving out to inch past them in the fast lane.

It was eleven forty-five when they turned into the long country lane which would lead, in a couple of miles, to the Marsh house. Joseph felt happier when Hastings said, 'Almost there' over his shoulder, and sat back to compose himself for the meeting. Being late had always given him the feeling of starting off on the wrong foot, of always being one apology behind in the exchanges which took place thereafter. It was an avoidable disadvantage, and one that he had resented on the rare occasions when it had been unavoidable.

As the car turned into the drive, he saw with surprise that there were two police cars by the house. There were several policemen standing round on the gravel, one of whom detached himself from the group and walked towards the car with hand outstretched. Hastings, using a shocked tone which amused Joseph, despite his growing concern, said, 'Sir Joseph has a luncheon appointment with Mrs Marsh, officer,' and the young face turned towards Joseph for a moment with a faint recognition. He said doubtfully, 'Just a moment, sir. I'll check with the officer in charge,' and walked quickly across to the group by the house.

A tall man with pips on the epaulettes of his shirt detached himself from the group and walked over. He had a harassed air and tired eyes, and seemed distracted. 'Could I have a few words with you, sir?' he asked, and Joseph levered himself out of the back seat of the car with difficulty, holding the door to pull himself upright. They walked round to the side of the house, out of earshot of the others, and Joseph noted that an ambulance stood there, the doors wide open. The tall officer began to speak in a low, intense whisper.

'I know you're handling the inquiry into Mr Marsh's death, sir. I'm afraid I have some rather shocking news. The housekeeper phoned us this morning, and we came round to find Mrs Marsh dead. There was a bottle of whisky and an empty bottle of tablets. They've been sent for analysis.'

Joseph looked at him. 'And the safe,' he said. 'Did you check the safe?'

The tired eyes gazed at him without comprehension. Very carefully, as though speaking to a foreigner, the officer said, 'There wasn't a break-in, sir. I think this one is an open and shut case. She couldn't live without her husband.'

Joseph was very quiet on the drive back. As the car neared Shepherd's Bush he took his list from his case and crossed through Lydia's name. After a few moments' thought he wrote the word 'appointment' against James Bergman's name.

Inappropriately, Hastings put the 'Hymn to Joy' on the car stereo. Joseph said nothing, knowing he meant well.

16

Grishkin walked down the long corridor, lined with the portraits of obscure officials painted in the heroic poster style approved by the party. He carried a briefcase and, in the other hand, a sheaf of papers. He paused in front of a massive oak door at the end of the corridor and licked his lips nervously before banging three times with his briefcase and pushing the door open with his shoulder.

Kalevsky sat at an ormolu desk in one corner of the great room. Despite being dwarfed by the sheer height of the windows, the massive scale of the whole room, he seemed to dominate the interior with his squat presence. He indicated the chair facing the desk with the end of his pencil, which he then used to tap his teeth. As always he said nothing, merely looking steadily at his subordinate with a disconcertingly direct gaze. Grishkin sat down, placing the briefcase by the side of his chair and the papers on the table. He felt nervous under the level gaze of Kalevsky's eyes.

He picked out a report and held it at arm's length. Really, he must start to wear his glasses. He had delayed doing so, outside his own apartment, because their use seemed to indicate some sort of weakness. 'Here, Comrade,' he said, holding out a report, but Kalevsky merely put the paper on the pile of documents in the tray on the right-hand side of the desk and said, 'Tell me.'

Grishkin poured himself a glass of iced water from the decanter on the table. He felt annoyed at himself for feeling so nervous, particularly since the report indicated that everything had gone according to plan. 'Well, Comrade. We set up the situation as planned. Our operative followed the man and the target into the country where he observed them embracing in a field. Later he followed them to the man's flat where sexual congress undoubtedly took place between the man and target. As you know, we were advised that Sir Joseph Sainsbury had been appointed to conduct a Commission of Inquiry into Marsh's death. We also discovered from our sources that Marsh had left a note. Our operative's instruction was to delete target in such a way as to suggest suicide, but also to carry out an apparently unsuccessful attempt to break into the safe. The object, as you know, was to maximize the element of scandal and increase pressure on the Commission of Inquiry to force disclosure to the public of information regarding experiments being carried out at Porton Down. The secondary aim being that public pressure to discontinue such experiments, and American concern, would render these experiments inoperative, take them out of the negotiating process.'

Kalevsky said, 'Well? Has anything happened to suggest that your plan has succeeded?' His voice carried the unmistakable overtones of a sneer.

'Only that our man informs us that the death is rumoured to be an inside job by the Americans or the British. The official verdict has been suicide, of course, but we feel it unlikely that Sainsbury will accept that.'

Kalevsky said drily, dismissively, 'We now employ mind-readers, it seems.' But he asked no more questions, picking up some papers from the tray and putting them in front of him. It was his way of signalling that the interview was over. When Grishkin reached the door, Kalevsky looked up.

'Do they know about Alexandrevitch?' he asked, and Grishkin said, 'We don't know for sure, sir.' He wasn't going to volunteer any more suppositions. He was still smarting about Kalevsky's sneer about mind-readers an hour later.

17

Kagan was angry. It was not that Lydia's death bothered him in a personal – or moral – sense. It looked, though, like one of those pieces of gross inefficiency which were beginning to seem the hallmarks of both his department and Maskelyne's. It was never discussed at their infrequent meetings, of course. Maskelyne had been particularly abrasive about bad form in the past and, while the concept meant little to Kagan, he had become dimly aware of the areas to which it referred. And the rivalry between them had never been greater. But none of them had any confirmation that Kalevsky and his masters had taken the bait, Alexandrevitch seemed to have vanished into thin air, and now this. He half-suspected that it was one of Maskelyne's operatives trying to get to the safe, and to shut Lydia Marsh's mouth. He'd already had Sir Joseph Sainsbury on the phone, seeming to imply just that in a roundabout, Limey way, and he had been forced to trot out the innocent line again. 'It seems to be a police matter. Looks as though it was a case of the lady being unable to cope with her husband's death.' And he knew that Sainsbury was due to meet James Bergman today. That worried him. The reports indicated that Bergman and Marsh's widow had become more than just friendly. Even before all this, when Bergman had come to see him, he had appeared to be under enormous stress.

Kagan leaned back in his chair until the swivel hit the rest. He laced his fingers behind his head and gazed up at the ceiling. The blank, distractionless white helped him to think. Irrelevantly, a picture of his last meeting with Reinecke came into his mind, and he smiled at the memory. Just occasionally, he thought, the sun does smile on me. He'd gone to the Senator's suite after the official dinner on their first night in Geneva, sweating profusely in his crumpled dinner jacket. It had been fear and not heat this time, because he had to tell the Senator about the Commission of Inquiry. Reinecke would not be pleased, he knew. But, if the Senator had taken the bait he'd set up, the situation could be salvaged.

He doubted, gloomily, that the Senator would have dared to pursue the situation, given the fact that he was so much in the spotlight. He rang the bell and waited. He heard Reinecke's voice saying, 'That'll be service. Just a moment,' and the door opened to show the Senator in his shirtsleeves, with a blonde woman just getting off the bed to be out of sight of the door. Kagan relaxed. Everyone can be bought, he thought, smiling at the Senator. Reinecke had pulled the door shut behind him so that both men were out in the corridor, but not fast enough to prevent Kagan seeing that the lady was scantily clad and very pretty. He had smiled at Reinecke just enough to let the Senator know that he had seen but, what the hell, they were both men of the world. Reinecke had listened in silence while Kagan told him about the Commission of Inquiry. It had been pure pleasure to have him by the balls for once.

'I suppose there's nothing we can do?' Reinecke had inquired half-heartedly, looking hard at Kagan. And Kagan, for once in the role of dispenser of patronage, had said soothingly, 'Sir Joseph Sainsbury is an old wartime buddy of Maskelyne, sir. The British know how to tell lies in style.'

He didn't admit that things didn't seem to be working out quite so simply. Kagan knew that Sainsbury was a sick man.

Andre had confirmed that. It could be any time, apparently. Grimly, Kagan had begun to think that he might have to be pushed. Andre was a friend, and an amateur. No point in looking that way – unless, of course, there was evidence that Sainsbury was prepared to play the game. After he had said goodnight to the Senator and had gone back to his room, he began to reflect in earnest, though no real solution offered itself over the next few hours.

They had first been alerted by Joseph's continuing interest in Sally Kane. The tapes had just been a routine check, and the departments working in tandem had controlled that meeting, pretty much. But – and Kagan could never understand why Sainsbury had reached his conclusions – Sainsbury had begun to look for evidence of a child. (Avery had constructed an ingenious story to get the information from the filing clerk. He had invited her to a show. Later, she had waited for forty-five minutes outside the theatre in Shaftesbury Avenue, a little wistful towards the end. But he never came.) In itself the discovery might mean nothing, but Sainsbury had begun to show himself at odds with the department in too many ways to be entirely trusted. Kagan had gone through the tapes again and again to see if Sally, for some inexplicable reason, had given a hidden message, and had found nothing. Next time they'd have to use visual surveillance as well, he thought. He'd been trying to get the department to accept visual surveillance for years, without success.

He thought about Joseph Sainsbury for a long time. It was never easy with public figures. Then he picked up the phone and said to his secretary in the outer office, 'See if Brigadier Maskelyne is free for lunch later this week. And make it somewhere quiet, will you?'

18

James woke at four thirty. It took him a little while to realize that he was dreaming and that he was in his own bed, at home. In his dream he had been pursuing Anna through a devastated city. The buildings were broken scags of brick and concrete, gutted by some terrible catastrophe. The streets were full of abandoned cars. There was no sign of life apart from the two of them, and Anna ran ahead of him, clad in some diaphanous material which billowed behind her. Like a ghost she ran through the streets and up a long, ramped causeway which led to a black door. He ran behind her, wondering how she had managed to escape the boggy quicksand which sucked at his feet, and frightened that she was going to disappear and leave him alone. He called after her, 'Wait for me,' but the wraithlike form sped on with demonic energy. As it got to the door it turned, and he saw that it had no face. Then he awoke.

He followed a new regime now. Instead of lying in bed, prey to the memories and the remorse which had become such potent parts of his waking life, he got up and made himself a cup of tea. He had not even read the papers or listened to the radio or looked at television for three days now. It was hard, in this cocooned state, to feel that anything which happened outside the immediate purlieus of his own preoccupation was important. Sitting in his dressing-gown, unshaven, in the pale light of early dawn, he tried to reason out what he should do about Lydia Marsh. In the old days, before the questioning of his own attitude, the ethics of the department, the morality of what he had done and was about to do, had begun, it would have been simple. Tell Kagan and pass the responsibility to someone else. Now, disturbingly, he had begun to regard Kagan, Maskelyne and the others in a new light: to feel that the expediency to which they gave primacy was flawed and unimportant in the scheme of things. It was part of the new dimension he had uncovered in himself over the past few weeks.

Despite this, he was still not free enough of the demands of his old life, of the department, to believe that there could be any future for himself and Lydia. Faced with these broader issues, that analytical quality in himself which had in the past been an aid to making decisions had been modified, broken down, made uncertain by the events of the past few weeks. Sipping his tea in the silence, now punctuated by a few notes of birdsong, by the occasional passage of a car, he reflected that it was hard to see how he had accepted the simplistic doctrines of the department so wholeheartedly. That ethic, which taught that the individual is expendable in pursuit of objectives legitimized by the department, now had a sour, alien taste. Sometimes, at the edge of his mind, a brief memory of a body lying awry when the deed had been done returned to him in a subliminal flash. But his mind moved away from those memories. He was not strong enough to face them yet.

He went to the desk. Looked at the letter of resignation he had written. It had lain there for two days while he thought of the consequences of resignation. He felt afraid, suddenly vulnerable to the knowledge that he knew nothing else. It was hard to know what other work he could do, where else he could go. Yet he knew that he could never again assume that uncritical posture of acceptance towards the department's rules which alone afforded him a limited security. And he guessed that Carter might have intimated as much in his reports to Kagan. That was Carter's true *métier*, after all. The smiler with the knife under his cloak. The letter wasn't right, or the right thing to do. He tore it up.

He had not rung Lydia since taking her home three days before. It was strange – to desire her physically in this way, but to be held back by the knowledge of his complicity in what had happened. To go forward with her he felt he would have to tell her most of the truth. (How he still qualified, still held on to the shreds of secrecy . . .) That would break the rules, and would send her away for ever.

He had read and re-read the note he received from her the day after he had last seen her like a lovesick adolescent, searching for some permanent, reliable truth in what seemed to be happening between them.

> I feel guilty about what happened, but I feel it is something we both wanted and needed. Life goes on, as the old cliché says. I don't regret it for a moment, don't think that, but perhaps it is too soon to feel decent. Apart from David you are the only man I have ever known. I want to see you again, to know more about you, but the time is not right just yet . . .

And now he had been summoned to a meeting with Sir Joseph Sainsbury about Marsh's death. Carter had called on the scrambler, and there had been a thread of anxiety in his voice. 'You know the line,' he'd said. 'As the reports suggested, he was obviously devastated by the fact that his association with Sally Kane had got out. Couldn't take it.' Carter had seemed to be on the verge of saying something else, but James cut him short without ceremony. He could only remember Lydia's conviction that her husband could not have committed suicide. James wondered, too, how naïve he himself might have been, knowing only part of the plan. He recollected a meeting once when four of them had been briefed by Carter's predecessor, each knowing that the orders to terminate his contract had already been given. One forgot those things, or denied that they could ever apply to you. Now he found himself wondering what line he could take, should take. It was a strange sensation to be drifting thus, compassless, on a wide, untenanted sea.

He arrived at Sir Joseph's flat at five minutes to eleven. He'd managed to beat a large Daimler with smoked-glass windows to a diagonal parking space. The chauffeur had put his window down and launched on a furious monologue about people who stole parking spaces. James looked at him without speaking, deadpan, and put his money in the meter. He felt a subversive, unaccustomed delight in violating one of the primary codes of the Bureau: to do nothing which would in any way draw attention to one as an individual.

The same austere lady, crimped iron hair and gold-rimmed half glasses, who had answered the entryphone let him into the spacious flat and showed him into the sitting-room. He'd barely opened *Country Life* before she came back and announced that Sir Joseph would see him now. He followed her into the study.

The glimpse at Edward Reinecke's reception, the newspaper photographs, the coy descriptive copy, had not prepared James for the man in the flesh. He was grotesquely ugly, and his overweight frame moved with an amorphousness, the amoeba-like movements of a creature without a skeleton. But his grip was surprisingly firm, and he exuded an immense, animal warmth, like an affectionate dog who only wants to be loved.

Joseph said, 'You're a coffee man at a guess, Mr Bergman. That is, if you're like those compatriots of yours I've dealt with. Come in and sit down.' An easy man to like, James thought. Somehow the ugliness was endearing, perhaps because it conferred an immediate, spurious superiority on any other man in Joseph's company.

But when the questions began he realized that the warmth formed a part, but was certainly not the whole man. They were deceptive, asked with a benign, twinkling jollity, as though to suggest the answers really weren't that important. But underneath James saw that they were relentless and probing, touching on matters of which he knew little, though he had speculated upon them. What secrets might Marsh have had? What was Alexandrevitch's status, and where was he now? James felt more confused than ever. In the old days he would have been instructed on his answers. He would have avoided making any comment at all about matters of which he knew nothing and, because the department worked on the cell system, he could justifiably have pleaded ignorance of almost every aspect of what happened. But now it was different. He even offered Sir Joseph information on the orders to 'take out' the two women at Porton Down. He was surprised when the other man looked up from his notes, fixing him with a look over his gold-rimmed glasses, and said quietly, 'One was your wife and Brigadier Maskelyne's daughter, wasn't she?' He felt a sense of relief, surmising that Kagan must have given the information. Ruefully, he realized that the rules must still apply to him, somewhere beyond the level of conscious thought.

It was when he thought the interview was over that Sir Joseph shocked him. He'd realized, instantly, that the brutality of the question was unintended. Sainsbury had just assumed he must have known. But James hadn't read the papers or heard the news for some days now.

'Can you shed any light on Mrs Marsh's death?'

The room seemed to spin around and a black mist rose before James's eyes. At first he couldn't really comprehend the question. He'd seen Lydia only a few days before. She couldn't be dead. And then he remembered the letter. He struggled to keep his voice steady.

'Was the safe tampered with?'

Sir Joseph made a note on the pad in front of him. Without lifting his eyes from the paper he said, 'I'm sorry. I hadn't realized you didn't know . . . ' Looking up, he continued, 'It seems that we think alike. That was the first question I asked the police. They haven't yet given me an official confirmation either way . . . ' After a pause he said, 'I suppose you wondered about the letter?' He patted the folder on his desk. 'Mrs Marsh sent it to me only a few days ago. It may have some part to play in the conclusions I reach.'

James stood up. His legs felt weak and he swayed unsteadily, reaching out to grab the arm of his chair. He said stubbornly, 'It couldn't have been suicide. She just wasn't the type.'

Sir Joseph smiled gently, without malice. 'Are you sure that's an objective evaluation? If I read matters correctly, you were becoming very close to her. By all accounts she was a very likeable person . . . '

It had to be the department, James thought. Rivers, perhaps, or Carter. Frightened when they were discovered looking for the letter. Aloud he said, 'Did you think there might have been an attempt to open the safe, sir?'

Joseph nodded. 'What bothers me most of all is that there had been an attempt that hadn't succeeded. And no pains had been taken to cover up the attempt. Almost deliberate, I would say . . . '

Afterwards, James stopped the car in Regent's Park and walked into the rose gardens. From the zoo came the faint sounds of a wolf howling. Suddenly, without warning, he found himself crying. He felt ashamed, but couldn't stop. How curious people were about lovers, about pain, about disaster. But it was a curiosity which contained a sense of relief. Nobody asked him what was wrong: they just looked at him and then went past, about their own business.

19

Joseph had begun to reminisce more, of late. Perhaps it was the foreknowledge of impending death which made him go back over his life, sifting it for meaning. Not the meaning conferred by other people: the knighthood, the honorary degrees, the newspaper eulogies, but some real and fundamental appraisal that would appease a hunger within him. After Honecker's disclosures he had begun to suspect that the chances of publishing the findings of his inquiry in full might be remote. Though there was still evidence to sift, he already saw a shape, and it was not a shape which would be readily acceptable in a report available to the public. He remembered the steps outside his door the previous night, and the sound as of the handle being gently turned. He had lain quietly until he heard the sound of soft footfalls dying away down the stair-well. It was not the event of death itself that he feared, but that he should not be able to complete his work. Perhaps his nightly barring and chaining of the doors had not been so fanciful, after all.

He felt lonely now in a way he had never felt lonely before. It was strange to realize it, knowing that he could invite any one of a dozen friends to dinner, or to a club, many of whom had known him since their days at Oxford together. That they could talk of their families, and the shared experiences of the past, and most subjects under the sun, with wit, and warmth, and good humour. The loneliness of what he was now doing presaged the loneliness of that other journey ahead. He picked up his watch. Five thirty. Still a long time before breakfast and the newspapers. He began to doze, propped among the pillows.

The incident in Berlin. That was what he had been trying to remember for some days past. He had gone with the Brigadier (then Acting Major) into the ruined city. Though the guns were still booming to the east they walked without care for themselves across the blackened rubble of destroyed buildings, past ragged groups of people who stood pitifully warming their hands before fires fed with pieces of wallpaper and old timber joists. Their faces all wore the same shocked, empty look. Then, round a half-demolished shoulder of wall, they had come across a group of Russian soldiers. Two of them were manhandling a blindfolded man to kneel in position by several others, facing the wall. They paid no attention to the two British officers. When the man had knelt alongside the others the soldiers rejoined their fellows, who stood in ragged formation a few yards away. A young man, barely twenty by the look of him, walked up to the prisoners with a pistol in his right hand. The two British officers watched in horror as he raised the pistol and put it to the nape of the first man's neck and pulled the trigger. The man fell forward against the wall, sliding down into a heap on the ground. The wall ran with blood. There was a smell of fresh cordite suddenly, rising above the reeky smoke of a thousand fires. Maskelyne moved forward holding out his hand. 'Stop,' he said, 'this is against the rules,' but the man only looked at him with a level gaze, and then moved on to the next prisoner. He pulled the trigger again, and the man fell heavily, his head snapping back.

Maskelyne fumbled with his revolver holster and Joseph said urgently, 'Sir, it will achieve nothing. The Russians have no regard for the Convention. They'd as soon kill us as well.' He had felt ashamed, he remembered, as though his intellect had betrayed his principles. Maskelyne again said, 'Stop,' and the young man looked up at him incuriously. In perfect English he said, 'If you need to know who I am for your report, my name is Kalevsky. Officer in charge, Unit Three.' He walked down the line and shot another man.

Joseph had drafted a report, but had never followed it up. Shortly after, he had been demobilized and then it was Oxford and the war was behind him for a few years – even in memory. When he first met Maskelyne, at a reunion party four years after the incident, he had tried to find out what had happened. But all Maskelyne would say, in his customary expressionless manner, was, 'I followed it up in my own way.' And now, as the pattern began to emerge, Joseph began to see the shape of what had been done. He felt sad at the waste, the acrimony, the bitterness. But men needed darkness as well as light to grow, he reflected.

It was James Bergman who worried him. Joseph and his wife had never had children, and lately Joseph had found in himself an instinct to look upon certain young men as the sons he had never had. It was to do with continuity, and – he had to admit it – a pride which had already begun to mourn the future loss of identity, the division of the spoils of his life amongst people who might remember for a year or so, and then no more. What quality in James evoked this instinct Joseph could not tell. Joseph realized that the boy (he snorted in self-derision for thinking of Bergman as 'a boy') must have done things which were abhorrent. That he had been obediently subject all these years to the dictates of a department whose doings had sometimes occupied a part in Joseph's past cases or his inquiries. In the ordinary course of things Joseph had no time for such people. Their spurious evocation of the interests of national security rarely held water on a close examination. Even George, he knew, bent the rules to suit his own purposes until the distinction between the security of the nation and the whims of the individual became blurred and tenuous.

The light had grown stronger as he reflected, glowing through the curtains. Almost time for breakfast. Then his chauffeur would pick him up to take him to Heathrow. He shouldn't have to spend more than one night in Berlin. He could have arranged for photostats over the phone, even had the details faxed to him. But Hans Biermayer was an old friend, and Joseph didn't want to involve anyone else in what he suspected was becoming a dangerous business. He smiled wryly to himself, reflecting that he was hardly the most capable person to take care of himself these days. An elderly lawyer with a diseased heart. When, during their bridge evening, two nights ago, he had told Andre he was flying to Berlin, his friend had been worried. 'It isn't my business to ask why you must go. But I beg you to send someone else, if you can.' He'd felt oddly comforted by Andre's concern.

In the plane he felt momentarily light-headed. The last time he had flown, so long ago, had been when Elaine had finally persuaded him to take a holiday. Despite his grumbling, his concern at the time about leaving the practice for a whole fortnight, he had found himself feeling like a child, full of excited anticipation. It had been like going to Southsea for the day, just after the Great War. 'You see,' she had said, 'you didn't know what you'd been missing all these years.'

Before the plane had left the runway he was nursing a large brandy. 'Only one,' he said in his mind to Andre, smiling at the recollection of his friend's worried features.

Back in tourist class Burberry sat with a briefcase on his lap. He thought about David Marsh's garden, and he felt a warm glow of satisfaction. In normal circumstances Avery or Carter would have been the right person for this assignment. But he was profiting by their past errors. It had been

Carter who briefed him, and Burberry had felt a strange, paradoxical surge of pleasure when Carter had said, 'Report only to me. Nobody else to be contacted. And if anything goes wrong, you're on your own.' Still, it had been strange that Rivers hadn't got the job. This would have been just up his street. It was difficult to sort out where orders came from in this new set-up. Vaguely he realized that there was some competition between the Americans and Maskelyne, but the politics were too far removed from him to engage his understanding or concern. He told himself that there would be a promotion if this went well. It took him half an hour to get a drink. But then, he wasn't a natural leader. He'd always known that.

PART TWO

1

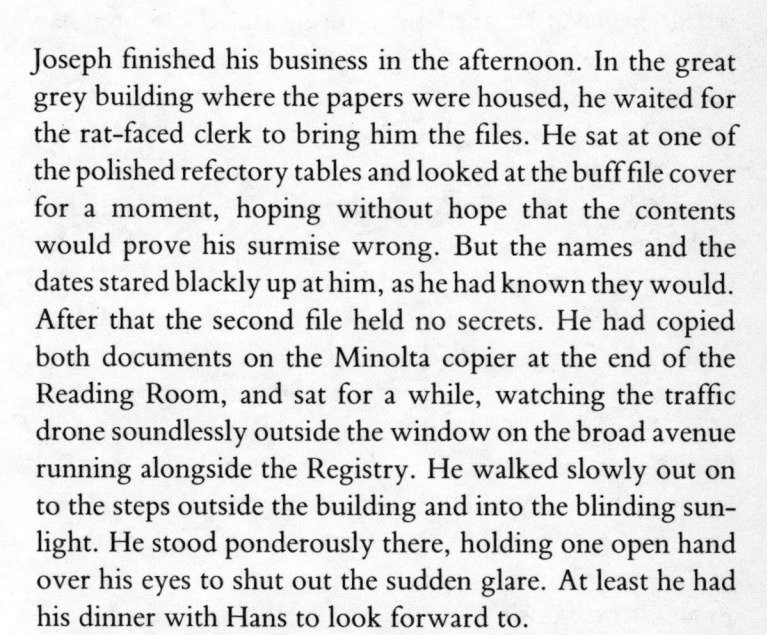

Joseph finished his business in the afternoon. In the great grey building where the papers were housed, he waited for the rat-faced clerk to bring him the files. He sat at one of the polished refectory tables and looked at the buff file cover for a moment, hoping without hope that the contents would prove his surmise wrong. But the names and the dates stared blackly up at him, as he had known they would. After that the second file held no secrets. He had copied both documents on the Minolta copier at the end of the Reading Room, and sat for a while, watching the traffic drone soundlessly outside the window on the broad avenue running alongside the Registry. He walked slowly out on to the steps outside the building and into the blinding sunlight. He stood ponderously there, holding one open hand over his eyes to shut out the sudden glare. At least he had his dinner with Hans to look forward to.

They went to a small restaurant on Friedrichstrasse. Hans was by himself. Grey now, thinner than Joseph remembered, but still as erect as when they had first met at Oxford. Greta had taken the children away for a holiday, he explained. It maintained the unspoken convention between them. Greta and Hans had dragged on together, year after year, for the sake of the children. Only once had Hans referred to it in any way. His first marriage to an Oxford girl had lasted only a year. 'To make a mistake once is forgivable. But twice . . . ' He threw up his arms in mock despair. 'What man could live with himself after such an acknowledgement?'

Hans was a doctor with a large and lucrative private practice. What few people knew was that he ran a clinic where he treated the poor free of charge, sometimes even paying for their medication from his own pocket.

It was pleasant to have a meal with an old friend who was totally unconnected with his present inquiries. But when they had finished their meal, and the waiter had brought them their coffee and schnapps and an artfully arranged bouquet of marzipan roses in the midst of which sat the bill, Hans said, 'Joseph, I know you and Andre are very old friends, but I think you should, perhaps, only consult him about health problems.' When Joseph had looked uncomprehendingly across at him, bewildered by the turn the conversation had taken, Hans leaned forward and patted his arm. 'It may be nothing at all,' he said, 'but Andre called me two days ago. He was very insistent that I should meet you at the airport. Accompany you wherever you were going. He would call me to check on your welfare. I was taken aback by his persistence. He seemed unnaturally anxious. He kept stressing that I should call him back to report. At first I felt like telling him that I couldn't possibly impose in this way on an eminent lawyer about his own business, even if he were a very dear friend. Then I remembered Andre's excitement one day when we were at college. He had been approached by a man called Hollis to carry out some intelligence work. He swore me to secrecy then and, to be quite honest, I had completely forgotten the matter for all these years. But I wonder about it now, and can't help thinking there may be more to his concern than a simple regard for your health.'

Joseph sat back in his chair. The diners had all left and

the waiters stood around with the attitude of men trying to suggest they had no interest in what time the restaurant closed. He picked up the bill, saying firmly, 'No, I insist,' slightly shocked at the size of it. When the waiter had taken it, swooping like a gannet to bear it away to the cash desk, he said, 'Don't bother yourself, Hans. I've known Andre as long as I've known you. I'm sure there's nothing to worry about.' But behind the simulated unconcern his mind had begun to work.

In the street Hans said, 'I'll give you a lift to the hotel,' but Joseph, relieved to be out of the restaurant, said, 'It's all right, my friend. A little exercise won't do me any harm. Give my love to Greta and the boys.' When Hans suddenly embraced him fiercely Joseph thought, he's a doctor, he must know that we won't see each other again, and was surprised by the sudden rush of affection he felt. *'Auf Wiedersehen,'* he said gruffly, and walked down the street without looking back. He was ashamed of the tears running down his cheeks.

After walking for a few minutes he felt tired. It wasn't the exercise, or even the needling pain behind the breastbone, but the growing certainty that Andre, too, had joined in the conspiracy. He mocked himself gently. What conspiracy? All that Andre had done, so far as Joseph could see, was to keep himself (and probably George) informed of his movements. Though, as Joseph realized only too well, even this might not prove to be a completely harmless activity.

He waited patiently by the lights. When the pedestrian signal changed to green he began to walk across slowly, still thinking about Andre. A white Mercedes suddenly appeared in the fast lane, moving at speed, and he realized instantly that he could not move out of its way fast enough. The car was heading straight for him and he found himself transfixed, incongruously, like a rabbit in a trap, mesmerized by the approaching headlights. A black car was racing up behind the Mercedes and, just as it seemed inevitable the Mercedes would hit him, the black car rammed it with such force that both cars veered up the central island. The Mercedes hit a lamp standard with a crash of rending metal and ended up on its roof, while the black car slewed to halt head-on against the bottom of the railing running down the central island. There was pandemonium. People got out of their cars and rushed to where the Mercedes lay, its wheels still spinning furiously in the air. Joseph stood rooted to the spot. The driver of the black car got out of his vehicle and moved slowly to the far pavement where he was soon lost in the crowd. Joseph, watching him go, was almost convinced that he knew the man. That he had thought of him as a son.

He walked over to the Mercedes. A man said to him in German, 'You were very lucky,' almost accusingly, and Joseph said, *'Ja. Ja. Danke,'* abstractedly, looking down at the torso of the man protruding from the driver's seat window. The thinning black hair was matted with blood and the open eyes were vacant, dead.

It took the police several minutes to arrive. Then he had to go with them and give a statement, half annoyed, half admiring their meticulous concern for detail. It was well past three when he finally climbed wearily into bed.

2

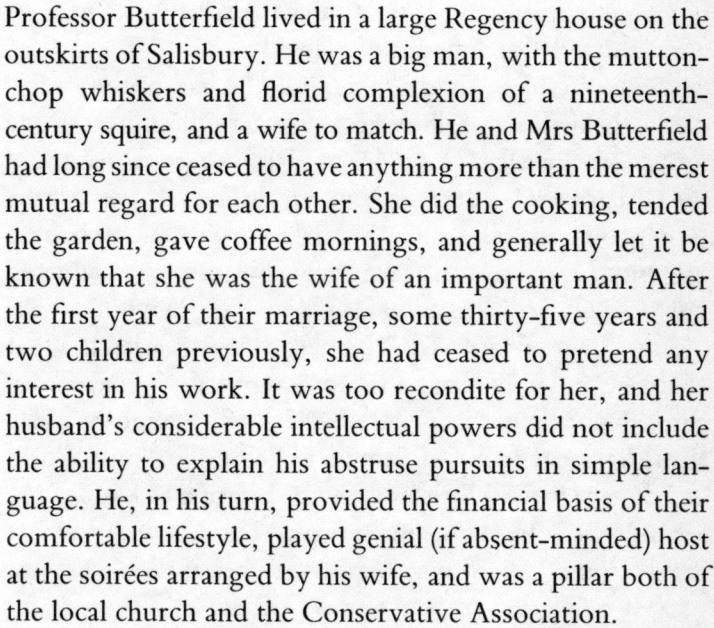

Professor Butterfield lived in a large Regency house on the outskirts of Salisbury. He was a big man, with the mutton-chop whiskers and florid complexion of a nineteenth-century squire, and a wife to match. He and Mrs Butterfield had long since ceased to have anything more than the merest mutual regard for each other. She did the cooking, tended the garden, gave coffee mornings, and generally let it be known that she was the wife of an important man. After the first year of their marriage, some thirty-five years and two children previously, she had ceased to pretend any interest in his work. It was too recondite for her, and her husband's considerable intellectual powers did not include the ability to explain his abstruse pursuits in simple language. He, in his turn, provided the financial basis of their comfortable lifestyle, played genial (if absent-minded) host at the soirées arranged by his wife, and was a pillar both of the local church and the Conservative Association.

It was an inadvertent remark by James Bergman which had led Joseph to arrange this appointment. When he had spoken to Butterfield on the phone he had formed the opinion that the Professor would have rejected the question of an interview out of hand if he had not been impressed by the fact that it was *Sir* Joseph Sainsbury who was requesting a meeting. An enraged Labour councillor had once accused him of hubris, but his interest in biochemistry was matched by his lack of enthusiasm for the classics, and he had grandly dismissed this as some obscure comment on his membership of the Tory Party. Sir Joseph's visit would no doubt provide Grace with fuel for her social chats over the weeks to come. Butterfield himself was sufficiently alert to wonder what the meeting might portend but, following a telephone call (made by him), and the conclusions reached in a meeting (arranged by them), he felt sufficiently confident and well prepared to view the prospect with his customary lofty equanimity. He knew that he could always invoke the provisions of the Official Secrets Act if matters appeared to be getting out of control.

None of which could explain why he had begun to feel distinctly nervous, following Grace's ample figure as she moved her kneeler from place to place along the margin of the herbaceous border, weeding assiduously as though the weeds had done her some personal injury. Walking behind her with his hands clasped over his bottom, he wondered uncharitably how he had managed to marry a woman with the most agonizingly trivial small talk in England. What could he possibly want to know about the Hendersons' party the other night, or how well the bring-and-buy sale at the Vicarage in aid of Famine Relief in the Third World had done? He felt a little ashamed at his own lack of feeling for his fellow humans, but consoled himself with the fact that he too espoused worthy causes, even if they were not so well publicized amongst his neighbours.

He saw Sir Joseph Sainsbury's chauffeur-driven Daimler coming up the sweep of the drive, past the acacias, to stop on the gravelled semi-circle in front of the house. 'Grace. Grace!' he called urgently, interrupting her latest story and causing her to sway back so that she could look back at him past her ample seat. 'He's here.'

While Grace walked as quickly as dignity would permit

through the french windows to wash her hands and arrange her thinning hair in the hall mirror, the Professor went over to the car to greet his visitor. The table by the willow had been laid in readiness for the past two hours, and Professor Butterfield knew that their daily, Mrs Hardy, would be taking the clingfilm off cucumber and cress sandwiches as he ushered Sir Joseph down towards the table.

Joseph raised an arm in the direction of the distant prospect of a sunlit spire. 'Is that the cathedral?' he asked, his face dappled with the sunlight breaking through the willow's dense fronds. Professor Butterfield, reassured by the innocuous and general manner of the question, talked eloquently about the cathedral and other local landmarks which he pointed out to his guest, like an Arab host extracting the choicest morsels for his visitor. Grace came down briefly, using her dignified walk with hands clasped in front of her, half curtsying to Joseph to his bemusement, and withdrew again to her gardening as soon as the pleasantries following her introduction had been exchanged.

When they were seated Joseph took a sandwich and bit into it appreciatively. 'I've a weakness for these,' he said, his confiding tone suggesting that they were just exactly the right choice. With his mouth half full he licked his fingers, wiping them on the napkin spread on his capacious lap, and said, 'How well did you know David Marsh?'

'Not well. I met him at a couple of official functions. We talked about general things . . . ' He trailed off uncertainly. This was not what he had expected.

'And did you meet a Russian gentleman called Pyotr Alexandrevitch at any of these functions?'

A vague sense of discomfort assailed Professor Butterfield. Annoyed with himself for the imprecision of the feeling, he picked up a sandwich and took a bite from it to give himself time to think. A blackbird hopped across the lawn with a sprightly bounce. From the corner of his left eye the

Professor saw his wife walk purposefully across the lawn with a pair of shears in her hand. The weathercock on top of the gable end of the roof veered uncertainly as the wind changed direction. He remembered the little Russian all right. They hadn't warned him about this.

He said guardedly, 'If he was the little man I met once or twice at David's parties, I can say I knew him by sight.'

Joseph noted the use of the first name. It confirmed his belief that the association had been closer than Butterfield would have him believe. He also noted Butterfield's use of the past tense when talking of Alexandrevitch. Did that mean that something had happened to Alexandrevitch? That Butterfield knew? He doubted that his next question would be answered any more honestly, but he had to try.

'And your speciality, Professor? I understand you were working on the auto-immune defence systems of the body when you were with the Cavendish. Correct me if I'm wrong, but I believe that your talents are being used in another direction altogether now?' He infused the question with a hint that he knew far more than he was prepared to admit, that the queries were really only to confirm something he already knew.

Butterfield began to panic. He felt indignant at being exposed to these questions without briefing. They had given him every assurance that he was protected from the authorities, that his involvement had the full sanction of government. Yet here he was, undefended and alone, having to venture into areas he suspected might be dangerous to him. He couldn't afford to appear in an official report at all, let alone in a dubious light. As always, he became pompous under the pressure of fear. He got to his feet, tipping the table with his knee, so that the Spode cups and plates fell with a loud crash on to the lawn. At the far end of the garden Grace looked up, startled, holding the shears aloft like a broadsword. The Professor was far too frightened even to apologize for his clumsiness.

'Now, look here,' he said. 'I think any other questions you may have should be put to me with my solicitor present.'

Joseph felt suddenly old and ill. It was important to show no weakness now, so he picked up his napkin from his lap and wiped it across his lips with quiet deliberation.

'I've no more questions,' he said. 'But I do have a comment to make off the record which you would do well to consider seriously. That is, that your present work may be in breach of your country's treaty regulations.'

Getting ponderously to his feet, he was surprised to see Butterfield smile. It was the smile of a man who possessed some secret talisman guaranteeing his immunity, who knew that he could not be held accountable for anything he had done. It contrasted oddly with the man's panic only a few moments before.

By the time Grace joined them by the car, Professor Butterfield's composure seemed quite restored. 'Sorry about the little accident, Sir Joseph. Sir Joseph will have to send us his dry-cleaning bill, won't he, dear?' And he laughed heartily at his little witticism.

He ignored Grace's pursed lips, and the little mutter under her breath in which the words 'the Spode' were the only recognizable ones. He watched the car disappearing down the drive, giving his genial hostly wave until it had vanished out of sight. Then Grace walked down to the willow where Mrs Hardy was already on her knees picking shards from the grass, and the Professor went into the house and up to his study. There was no need to lock the door, for no one dared to disturb him here. The horned owl in its glass case above the mahogany bookshelves glared down at him with its customary impersonal ferocity. He took off his jacket and hung it over the back of the captain's chair behind his desk. He undid his waistcoat and carefully removed the wire taped to the microphone which sat in his waistcoat pocket. Then took the spool from the miniature recorder taped inside the waistband of his ample trousers.

He picked up the telephone and dialled a London number. After four rings a voice answered and he said, 'Was that all right?' He listened for a moment and said, 'Good. Yes, I'll send the tape anyway.' When the tape was safely cached in a padded buff envelope, he relaxed. He was surprised to find himself trembling from head to foot. I've never really felt easy with people, he thought, watching Grace through the window as she traversed the lawn with a trug full of dead rhododendron heads. I've never really known how they work, or what they really want.

The thing which intrigued Joseph as he was driven back to London was the smile. Like Butterfield, he too felt that the facts were all that mattered. But the smile was a fact that didn't fit.

3

After Berlin, James knew there was no turning back.

He had heard from Carter that Sir Joseph was going to Berlin. Carter had called round without making any prior arrangement, as usual, and had lounged round the flat, picking up and examining ornaments with apparent curiosity. He seemed to be totally unaware of Bergman's unspoken hostility. 'When did you go to Japan?' he asked with apparently genuine interest, fingering a Japanese devil mask which sat on the long bookshelf lining one wall of the sitting-room. 'Portobello Road, 1954,' James said shortly, already tired of the oblique approach so favoured by the department.

Carter had already quizzed him about his meeting with Sir Joseph. Normally it was standard procedure to be wired, and to pass over the tape together with a written report for the analysts and psychologists to pore over. It was a double check on performance, to see if the operative had noticed and analysed the possible significances of a pause, an intake of breath. James had dispensed with both the tape and the report, and both Maskelyne and Kagan seemed to have accepted his maverick attitude with surprisingly good grace. Technically, of course, with the latest equipment they could easily have taped the conversation without his help.

James had begun to wonder just how far he could go before he incurred the Bureau's displeasure. There had, of course, been the mendacious proposal that he should follow Alexandrevitch to Moscow. He couldn't accept the line that his visit would be so obvious that Kalevsky's men would dismiss it as of no consequence, though the idea had a spurious believability about it. Now, after the deaths of Anna and Lydia, he had begun to perceive his past as corrupt and childish, as dealing with shadows, without responsibility; as being without some quality of reality which he now saw for the first time, prised loose from his past and dealing with the shopkeepers and traders of Haverstock Hill as an ordinary citizen. From this vantage point he saw an entire new dimension which had escaped him previously. Then (he supposed) his mind had been cluttered with the principles of the department which showed only contempt for ordinary people. Then, in the past, that secret contempt had lain in his mind during the dinner parties, the social engagements, where the wearying pretence of some sort of normal life must be maintained. He had been given a sophisticated brief for the job he purportedly held, which would stand the most rigorous scrutiny. Not that it mattered, anyway. You and the enemy knew each other's faces: the public didn't matter.

Carter had merely said in passing as he left, 'I gather your fat friend is going to Berlin on his excavations. The department's mystified,' and had let himself languidly out through the door. And James had known that, if the department had considered the situation enough to profess themselves mystified, there would be someone else on the plane with Sainsbury. Without thinking things out with any degree of clarity he felt an instinctive, jubilant certainty that the department had made the wrong choice in suggesting Sir Joseph Sainsbury to undertake the inquiry. That their attempts to head him off would be useless. And he knew that such men were dangerous to the department.

He had finally discovered Sir Joseph's flight from a less than discreet booking clerk at the Lufthansa desk at Heathrow. Knowing that he would be instantly recognizable to anyone from the department, he had taken the previous flight and had then waited by the Flight Arrivals entrance, suitably muffled to disguise himself despite the warm weather. Sure enough, he had spotted Burberry picking his way through the crowd with ferret-like anxiety. In the event he need not have bothered that he might be recognized. On this, his first big assignment, Burberry had eyes for no one but his intended victim. In his mind he carried the regulation case. James had assessed that Burberry would not use the dismembered rifle, cached under an X-ray diffuser in the false bottom of the case, unless some more obviously accidental method failed. Another rule of the Bureau was, 'Use the statistics' – which, being interpreted, meant that road accidents, cardiac arrests and strokes were favoured over the more flamboyant and traceable methods.

He had trailed Burberry's taxi to the hotel, keeping a hundred yards behind in his hired black Opel. Burberry had checked in, and James had followed him in another taxi to the Hertz office. James had never rated Burberry, but he was impressed by the touch. Burberry had eschewed the easy course of arranging the car through the hotel. If he used the normal disinformation procedures it would be days before the police connected the car with the middle-aged Englishman, by which time Burberry would long since have returned home.

It had involved much sitting in the parked Opel reading an assortment of local papers while keeping a covert watch. But Burberry seemed to have no thought that he too might be followed. The white Mercedes had been another professional touch. Usual accident contracts sanctioned by the Bureau in Germany would be done by a Polo or, at its most expensive, a Golf. By now he had no doubt it would be a road accident. He had trailed Burberry throughout the day, half surprised by this sudden instinct to protect Sir Joseph. He had followed Burberry's car to the records office, and then down to the Friedrichstrasse. He had watched Joseph and a thin, grey-haired man go into the restaurant. Time to wait. He watched the people passing by, tired now of reading. He reflected, with uncharacteristic thoughtfulness, that he had begun to pay for his past.

He had been half dozing when the Mercedes accelerated away from the kerb. He could see no sign of Joseph. He gunned the engine into life and sped after the other car, cursing himself for losing concentration. Four hundred yards down the wide carriageway ahead he suddenly saw Joseph Sainsbury begin to walk across the road with the ungainly gait of the overweight man. He pressed his foot to the floor, and the engine screamed, pushing the seat into the small of his back as the fuel injection took up. He accelerated out of the slow lane into the middle. In front the Mercedes was speeding down the fast lane. If he managed to hit it just right he could tip it over. If not . . . Joseph Sainsbury would be just another hit-and-run statistic.

It worked. As the Opel hit the rear of the Mercedes, Burberry threw a terrified glance over his shoulder. The wheel twisted in James's hands and he concentrated on bringing it to rest, aware of the Mercedes turning over and skidding on its roof, showering sparks across the black macadam. Now came the part he had rehearsed. To walk away without hurrying. The car was hired in a false name, using papers from the department files. But they were old ones, and he doubted the department would ever make the connection. Even the mandarins, endlessly picking over the entrails of what had happened and what was yet to come, would probably treat it as a contract which failed for reasons outside the operative's control. An accident. The report would just read that Burberry had made a mess of an assignment. He doubted that the department would even bother to send anyone out. Most probably it would be poor mousy little Elsa who would accompany her husband's body back to its last resting-place in Edmonton.

He thought Sir Joseph might have recognized him. He suspected that the lawyer had a shrewd idea by now of what was going on, would have realized that whatever he found could be construed as jeopardizing the aims and operations of the department.

He slept on the flight to Heathrow. Driving back, he felt strangely dislocated from his surroundings. There were a few circulars waiting on the mat. A *Hampstead and Highgate Express*. Nothing personal.

The next day he expected to get a call from Sir Joseph's secretary, the dry-as-dust tones asking him to come to a meeting. But nothing came. Finally, three days after his return, he called Joseph's number in the evening. It was a long time before the receiver was picked up, and he could hear the other man's stertorous breathing. Sainsbury only said, 'I've been expecting your call. I think we should meet as soon as possible.'

4

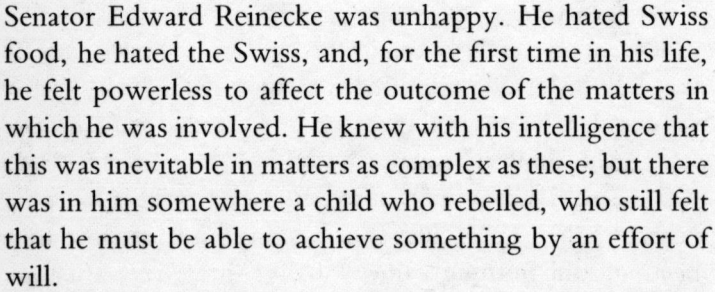

Senator Edward Reinecke was unhappy. He hated Swiss food, he hated the Swiss, and, for the first time in his life, he felt powerless to affect the outcome of the matters in which he was involved. He knew with his intelligence that this was inevitable in matters as complex as these; but there was in him somewhere a child who rebelled, who still felt that he must be able to achieve something by an effort of will.

He was having dinner with Helga at her flat in the suburbs of Geneva. She seemed to have accepted his abstraction and grumpiness, and had ceased to try to amuse him with light conversation. It was the first time in a month that they had not ended up in bed together before dinner, and her pride was hurt. She had never palled so quickly, and she had begun to feel uncertain of her powers of attraction. Looking through the door from the kitchen to where he sat, toying with his *apfelstrudel*, she wondered if she was getting too old for this sort of thing. True, she was well paid for the job, but she was thirty-six now, and it had become harder to simulate the ardour, to take care to hold in the stomach and brace her shoulders so that her breasts looked uplifted and youthful. During the past year she had often found herself thinking wistfully, if vaguely, of a larger apartment in a more fashionable suburb, of a shadowy husband (who, as it happened, bore some resemblance to the Senator), and a baby. It was the baby who appeared most clearly in her fantasies, a secret longing which had grown upon her over the past few months until it bordered on an obsession. She was a simple girl from a small village, who had few resources. She could not imagine how she would fill her later years without a child to look after. She had reached into her own life as far as she could, which was not very far, and her resources had run dry.

She watched Reinecke get up from the table and stand at the window in his shirtsleeves, smoking. In the street below, the anonymous black cars with their smoked windows and anonymous crews sat under the orange lights, awaiting the Senator's return from taking his pleasures. As she had wondered about other powerful men, she wondered if the Senator ever felt worried about the possible consequences of this liaison. Though he, of course, would have no idea of what was in her mind.

For the past ten nights she had taken no precautions. In a sense it had not been a deliberate decision, for she was not a person who could take decisions, but rather a gamble with the future. She had just become tired of waiting for the right man to come along. She sometimes remembered Benny, with whom she had lived for three years before she started this, with nostalgia. He had gone when he found out about the other men. She couldn't understand it. 'But they don't mean anything,' she had said, almost crying with exasperation as he packed in silence. Now all the men she met on these assignments were married, and she knew that she was only there to provide them with temporary pleasure, could never wean them away from their solid, bourgeois homes, their boring wives. Now she felt a secret, unfocused pleasure and anticipation in the fact that she was three days overdue.

She went into the dining-room and put her arms round

his neck and kissed his nape. He said thickly, 'Not here, Helga,' but she knew that the irritation, the abstracted air, were only superficial. He turned and took her in his arms, kissing her hard on the lips and moving his body against hers. She led him into the bedroom.

When she asked him afterwards – so casually that she could have been making an observation about the weather – how it was going at the talks, he moved away from her abruptly to the other side of the bed as though she had struck him. It was impossible, he said. How could he deal with people who were paranoid about American intentions, who could not realize that America, too, only wanted peace? How could they complain about American adventurism in Central America and the Gulf when their own troops were still firmly installed in Afghanistan? He sat on the bed and she let him talk, feeling that she was an irrelevancy here, that he was now talking to himself. She sensed a growing bitterness in him as he talked of past failures: of Kissinger, of Paul Nitze, of the others who had spent years in trying to hammer out some *modus vivendi* which might reduce the chances of nuclear war. By now back in bed with a cigarette clamped between his teeth, he reflected bitterly that he had long since realized that it was only a numbers game. That one had to envisage a complete absence of general goodwill, and recognize that self-interest, the will to cheat without being discovered, the desire secretly to hold the balance of power while apparently seeking equality, were all undeniable factors in the Warsaw Pact negotiating position. And, he added, for all he knew the same factors operated on the American side, though, he said hastily, he had no evidence of that. Then, almost as an afterthought, half under his breath, 'And now I understand there is a new British position to complicate matters,' and she was instantly alert, knowing she could not, dare not, say anything yet.

Later, while he was dressing, she lay with her hands behind her head (giving her breasts a youthful appearance) and said ingenuously, 'So the British have come up with something new,' trying to make the inquiry sound as disinterested as possible, and knew immediately that she had made a mistake, watching his body stiffen. 'I shouldn't have mentioned that,' he said shortly, and she watched him finish dressing in silence. A few minutes later he left. She lay there, suddenly lonely, thinking that it was the first time he hadn't made an arrangement to see her again. She felt sad, despite the foetus beginning to quicken in her womb.

At twelve-thirty she went to the white telephone on the wall in the kitchen and dialled a long number. Waiting, she felt a confusion of loyalties, but her way of life, her habit of accepting instructions, was too entrenched to permit her any sense of responsibility. After all, what she was about to do would not affect him personally, she thought. It might only mean, at worst, that he could fail to achieve some abstract, general principle. Such things were beyond her concept of reality. She spread her fingers against the white wall and examined her nail varnish while the phone continued to ring. They were taking a long time tonight.

When she identified herself to the voice on the other end she waited for the questions, as always. Nothing new to report, except a vague reference to 'the new British position'. Yes, she was sure he had used those words. She fancied there was a longer pause than usual before the next question, but didn't ponder it further. They paid her well, so what she said must be important. Neither of which reflections made her feel any better.

Back at the hotel, Edward Reinecke sat in a spoon-backed chair by the dressing-table, smoking. Kagan, leaning against the mock Sheraton table with a glass of bourbon in his hand, reflected that he didn't much like the Senator's taste in pyjamas. But what did that matter? He didn't like anything about the Senator. Watching Reinecke, he suddenly had to stifle an absurd desire to giggle. There was something faintly ridiculous about the whole situation.

He said soothingly, 'You did well, sir. It sounds as though the seed was well planted.'

Reinecke said, 'What happens to her now?' And Kagan thought, I could almost swear the bastard has a heart sometimes.

'Well,' he said, 'the most effective technique would be a termination which Kalevsky could trace to us. That would make it seem we were really worried.'

'No,' Reinecke said. He was surprised at himself. Why did he care? But some memory of her hair spread upon the pillow, her warm body beneath his, had touched some sunken part of him. He lifted a finger and pointed it at Kagan. 'And if anything happens to her I'll make sure you get yours. See to it.' The smile didn't reach his eyes.

Walking down the corridor towards his humbler room, three floors above, Kagan wondered what had happened. It was unlike Reinecke to let sentiment get in the way of expediency. He went into the room and turned on the light. It made a stark contrast with the acres of blue and gold splendour of the Senator's suite. He lay on the bed and looked up at the ceiling. Betty Reinecke wouldn't know about this, he thought, and his mind, ever accustomed to seeking advantage, began to ponder what patronage Reinecke might be prepared to offer under a little pressure.

5

Despite the urgency, Sir Joseph couldn't meet James for two days.

Since Burberry's death, James's sense of insecurity had grown. When he took his washing down to the launderette in England's Lane he would stop suddenly and look back over his shoulder. Or after a late dinner at La Baita, or the wine bar, he found himself looking suspiciously at everyone who passed him as he walked down Haverstock Hill. But nobody followed him. Carter never called. It was only the monthly pay cheque from International Enterprises, with its accompanying pay slip showing deductions, dropping through his letter box in its buff envelope which reminded him of his connection with the department.

His sense of aimlessness had increased. For him, whose life had been governed by the inflexible rules of the department for so many years, the freedom was frightening. Almost he found himself wishing for the assassin in the shadows, some tangible threat against which he could pit his armoury of skills. Without any such signs of the department's displeasure, without any call for expiation, he began to feel dispossessed of his persona, of some comfortable, safe, regular placement in the world. Now, when he went to a meeting of the housing cooperative to discuss the repainting of the house, he felt curiously naked, a hollow sham without the substance of a real job and a real life behind him. The cord he had cut which tied him to the department seemed to have severed his connections with his fellows, too. Love, the bonds of friendship, had all decayed and fallen away.

At night he was visited by pictures of Anna as he had last seen her. Of Lydia at their last meeting, here in the very bed where he now lay alone. The pictures came spontaneously, with a disturbing lack of emotion, so that they seemed to pose some cryptic question. He did not know what the question was, nor where the answer might lie, and he wished he could void the pictures from his mind.

In so far as he had thought about his religious beliefs at all since leaving college, he had identified himself, when asked, as an atheist. Now that the shadow had reached into his own life he felt afraid. Prompted by some volition of which he was half ashamed, he would draw the curtains and kneel beside his bed to say his prayers, as he had when he was a child. 'God be merciful unto me, a sinner,' he would begin, looking through his latticed fingers at the reproduction of Picasso's 'Mother and Child' on the opposite wall.

But it was superstition only. It reminded him of the dense, magical life of childhood. Of avoiding the cracks between the paving slabs. Of crossing your fingers when you told a lie. Of the whole host of supernatural allies, the apostrophizing of Fate and Life which, like others, he invoked to remove guilt and responsibility for his own actions. But now he knew. He knew that he bore some responsibility for Anna's death and more for Lydia's. He knew that to take no decision was to take a decision to do nothing. He knew that those deaths were the inescapable consequences of his own actions, and that there was no sanctuary where he could hide from what he had done. He saw Burberry's death as some positive attempt to right the balance. Or, to be more accurate, he saw that Burberry's death had been necessary to save Sir Joseph Sainsbury, who alone was in a position to set matters right. So far as they could ever be set right.

He had begun, too, to resume the training he had received when he first joined the department. Late at night, with the curtains drawn, he would practise his entry into the sitting-room, pretending it was a hostile environment in which some potential danger lurked. ('Ninety per cent of the time hostile will shoot through a door at between three foot six and five foot six. Avoid that area . . . ') He hung a bolster in the doorway with his dressing-gown cord. For ten minutes each evening he worked at it. One hand after another. Fingers extended and sinking deep into the target. Or the heel of the hand to the chin, or under the nose; the edge of the hand to the throat, or under the nose. The old images in the mind. The Viet Cong who was going to rape your daughter. The asiatic who would kill you unless you killed him first. The enemy . . . the enemy . . . the enemy. Sometimes, for a fleeting second, he would see Carter's sneering features, the languid, supercilious blond face superimposed on the yellow face of the enemy.

But no one followed him. No one phoned. His sense of isolation increased, day by day, hour by hour. Now he was terrified of missing the news. His television stayed on from the first broadcast in the morning until the epilogue, and the vanishing dot of light dwindling in the centre of the screen. It gave him some sense of the comforting cadences of human voices, though it never held his attention for more than a few seconds.

It was with a sense of relief that he prepared himself for his meeting with Sir Joseph Sainsbury. It was action of a sort, after all, he reflected, sorting through his wardrobe to choose a grey suit with a light pinstripe and a cream shirt. Somewhere he felt that the ugly, shambling figure of the lawyer possessed some magical strength, some hope to penetrate and cripple the arrogant invulnerability of the department. Undoubtedly they were worried about what he might discover. Burberry's presence on the flight proved that, surely? Though he suspected that Burberry had exceeded his brief. After all, had the department so intended, they could have come up with something in England. Briefly, he wondered who had instructed Burberry.

He knotted his tie and examined his face in the mirror. Hair neatly brushed, the wary grey eyes, the thready white lines scoring through the sunburn to bracket his mouth. Beyond that there was no visible sign of the pain of the past months.

It was late afternoon. He had been invited for the cocktail hour, when Sir Joseph's staff would have left for the day. The street was empty of pedestrians. He pressed the bell and gave his name softly into the grille by the door in response to Sir Joseph's voice. The ancient lift jerked him to the third floor.

He paused on the landing outside the flat door, looking with unseeing eyes at the last rays of sun catching the top of the building opposite. The window panes shone a brilliant red gold. As he went to ring the bell he wondered if this visit would prompt the department into action. He rang the bell and waited.

He was shocked when Sir Joseph opened the door. The dog-like, jowled face had a waxen pallor through which the liver spots of age showed clearly, and his breath had a sour, carious smell. At first James thought it must be drink, as Joseph seemed unsteady on his feet, but he suddenly remembered Carter saying, in that airy, who-cares manner of his, 'He's terminally ill, of course.' He felt sad, following the lawyer into the study. Such feelings had returned recently, and he found them confusing and messy. Joseph sat down heavily by the desk and shook out a pill into his hand. He indicated the drinks cabinet.

'Help yourself. There's some Jack Daniels on the second shelf.'

James poured himself a careful measure and sat down in an armchair opposite his host. The feeling of sadness persisted and, with it, a sense of wanting to protect the lawyer. When his father was dying he had felt the same. He looked at the massive figure slumped in the chair, the eyes closed and a light beading of perspiration on the forehead, and found himself saying with childlike directness, 'I'm sorry, sir. I understand you're very ill.'

The eyes in the big face looked at him. 'You heard from Andre, I suppose? Dying is the accurate description.'

James said awkwardly, 'I don't know who Andre is, sir. I heard it from Carter.' He put his glass down on the lace coaster.

'Kagan's supercilious lapdog? That makes sense . . . ' Joseph brooded a while, and then said, 'You saved my life in Berlin, didn't you? Please accept my tardy thanks. And now, perhaps you can tell me why?'

Something broke in James then, and he found himself telling the older man everything. About his marriage to Anna, his work for the Bureau, the terrible assignment when he had discovered, too late, that he had been set up to kill his own wife, Lydia's death, his own suspicions. As he spoke Joseph nodded from time to time, and James knew that everything he said was understood by the other man and provided some slight shift in focus affecting the facts the lawyer already knew.

Joseph got up and put the lamps on, moving slowly, his breathing laboured. He refilled James's glass. Everything he did possessed a precision, a quality of watchful concentration, which gave the impression that he missed nothing. Once he asked if James knew who had set the operation up:

Marsh's death, the other deaths? It had never occurred to James to consider it might be anyone other than Kagan because, despite the dual key, special relationship propaganda, it was undoubtedly the Americans who were in control of all major aspects of strategic nuclear policy in the UK. Sainsbury, in awkward movement again in search of peanuts, his half glasses perched on the end of his nose, had stopped, observing with a sly smile that there was no need to feel so apologetic about facts which were fully accepted by the Whitehall mandarins, even if it were felt unwise to spell matters out clearly to the electorate through the media.

Seated again, he asked if James had any idea of what information David Marsh might have had, or what security threat he might have posed. James took a deep breath, thinking, here goes, and said that it must be important, whatever it was, because in his estimation both Marsh and his wife had been silenced by the department.

But what about the letter in the safe, Joseph persisted. With the close ties between the police and the department it would have been a simple matter to get hold of the letter, if they had wanted it.

In the past James had never asked questions. Now he could only see puzzles, whichever way he looked. The fact that one of the operations had involved terminating Maskelyne's daughter, and that Maskelyne still seemed not to know, had not seemed to surprise Joseph. Acting devil's advocate for a moment, Joseph had only half convinced him with his rejoinder that it was after all a covert operation with both sides working in loose tandem, though separately. The identity of the girls was not important because, for the sake of speculation, Moscow already had their bishop in Marsh. So the papers had not identified the girls on instruction, and the internal reports had been glossed over to save the Brigadier's feelings. A strange picture had come into James's mind for an instant, then: Anna, standing in front of the altar in the church where they had been married, facing him with her right hand raised in the blessing. But Joseph was waving his large hand dismissively and saying, 'Coincidences are the very stuff of life,' and James had to be content with that.

In other ways Joseph had been open and accepting. Yes, he realized that the department may originally have felt that he would tailor his report to their needs, and that Burberry's trip, assuming it had been officially sanctioned, must indicate that they had become more concerned. 'Who would have briefed him?' he asked, and James replied, 'Any one of a dozen senior officers,' but his instinct said 'Carter', without any facts to support it.

They sat in silence for a little while. Joseph said sombrely, 'I wish I had never taken this on. Nothing good can come of it . . . ', and a few moments later, almost to himself, 'The one thing nobody realized, for all their cleverness, was that I couldn't be bought. Not with money or honours, certainly, but not even with spurious appeals to my sense of patriotism, or to national security . . . ' Deep in his throat he made a sound which could have indicated disgust.

It was a painful new world he had delineated for James. One in which there were higher appeals than expediency, where the absolute rightness of the Bureau seemed suddenly suspect, where the path of choice between the interests of the department and those of the country and of ordinary people had become distorted and wavering. He longed for his old certainties to return again. It was still strange, even after all that had happened, to have lost so irrevocably the protection of those limited tenets by which the department operated. Looking at Joseph, he found himself thinking: if I killed him they would accept me back, and things would be as they were before.

Joseph said simply, 'I felt from the first I would be able to rely on you. You don't fit there any more, do you?'

The moment had passed. He felt ashamed now, looking at Joseph's eyes regarding him. The unsureness had not gone, but merely sunk beyond recall for the moment. 'You must take care, sir,' he said, confused, still slightly ashamed of the sentiment of caring. And later, just before he left, he said, 'I'm frightened, sir. Are you ever afraid?' And Joseph had looked at him with a tired smile and said, 'My fears have changed over the years, but I have learnt to live with them every waking moment.'

On the way down the stairs James felt contrite. What had he to fear which compared with that grim sentence of death? He looked up from the street at the windows, but the glass was black, betraying no light. Back in his flat he felt restless, uncertain. He realized that he didn't know what he was going to do, or even what he wanted to do. His whole life had become uncertain.

6

Maskelyne sat in the club lounge waiting for Kagan. Irritably he lifted his cuff to look at his watch. He found other people's lateness insulting, as though it were a disparaging comment on his importance. But Kagan was always late. It seemed to give him the feeling of some power, some control over events. Maskelyne picked up the *Financial Times* in his white, bloodless fingers and glanced at his stocks. They were reassuringly buoyant.

As ever, Kagan made no apologies when he arrived fifteen minutes later. His brown pinstripe suit was crumpled and his cream shirt had a soiled, crinkly collar. He smelt acridly of sweat, mopping at his forehead with a rag of handkerchief. He shouted loudly at a passing waiter, who took his order impassively. 'And another . . .?' he gestured questioningly in the direction of Maskelyne's drink, but the other man shook his head at the waiter with his dry, distant smile.

'Jeeze,' Kagan said disgustedly, 'why don't we use the Mirabelle or Stringfellows for a change?' He still felt nervous and irritable after his trip to Geneva. While he had Reinecke by the balls he hadn't anticipated how tough the Senator could still make things.

At dinner Maskelyne had the bresaola followed by a Dover sole and a half bottle of Sancerre. Kagan had ordered the hamburger with another double bourbon, oblivious of Maskelyne's ironic glance. He seems totally unaware of what should be done, Maskelyne thought, the sense of superiority bolstering him for the conversation ahead.

By the time the dessert had arrived (profiteroles for him, jam roly-poly for Kagan) Maskelyne felt completely in command. Earlier Kagan had attempted to steer him into talking about the situation, but Maskelyne had merely remained silent, enjoying the other man's frustration.

Neither would admit to the other a confusion over Burberry's assignment. The briefing had never been minuted, and both, independently believing the other responsible, had accepted the outcome pragmatically, as something which was past recall. Carter had ventured the suggestion that Burberry may have misconstrued an off-the-cuff remark, but that didn't really wash. Neither side encouraged individual enterprise outside the established procedures, and Burberry had been nothing if not a born employee. It certainly was a mystery, but not worth further pursuit.

Watching Kagan unobserved, George Maskelyne thought, not yet, still preoccupied with the problem of explaining what was going on without it seeming a mistake, a failure on his part. Nor did he want Kagan to seek any advantage, to take control now, just because Burberry had been one of George's boys. It had become much harder to run a tight ship with the confused command structures and, he had to admit, the struggle for control. But there were important old loyalties, ways of doing things between old comrades-in-arms and, yes, friends. He didn't want the control over what had now become a necessity to slip from him this time, for matters to be carried out with the summary dispatch, the lack of decorum, which he saw as characterizing the American operations.

They had talked about Reinecke, and George had been

surprised by Kagan's reticence. Well, Kagan said, avoiding George's eye, the Senator had cooperated fully, as one would expect from someone with his responsibilities. Maskelyne thought cynically that Kagan might get up and sing 'The Star Spangled Banner' at any moment. He was certainly holding something back, that was evident. And using this *ersatz* display of patriotism to fudge the issue.

And the girl, George asked, had she been disposed of? (A hard fact, independently verifiable, no slipping out of this one.) Kagan had muttered inaudibly, looking uncomfortable. That must be it, Maskelyne surmised, wondering whether it was Reinecke or Kagan who had countermanded the original plan. They'd used Helga once, themselves. The photographs of her and the Soviet chief negotiator three years before had caused quite a stir. The fact that the plan had been altered gave Maskelyne a sense of security. It traded off against his own lapse into sentiment, made it more understandable. At least he had followed all the guidelines, so far. Nothing could be written into the records to suggest otherwise.

It had been difficult to sort things out with Burberry's widow. All that crying and twisting of her hands at first. She'd looked like some little charlady from Bethnal Green, with her thin, mousy hair and work-roughened hands. But later, surprisingly, she had asked some very canny questions about his pension rights and what she should say to the newspapers. He shifted in his chair, remembering how difficult it had been to feign indifference. But in the end she had seemed satisfied enough.

The Berlin police had been no problem. If Burberry hadn't taken the case containing the gun (without authorization) the department could have let the situation alone. He wondered, again, who had briefed Burberry. Perhaps, considering his status, he had merely been instructed to watch and report. This new generation thought too much for themselves. And perhaps, given the dual command structure, this had been something which fell between the cracks.

They were in a corner banquette, well away from the other diners, so that there was no danger of being overheard. When the dessert came, Maskelyne said, carefully choosing his words, 'I think we may have a problem with Joseph,' feeling a sense of irritation as he saw Kagan regarding him with a slight, superior smile. 'But,' he said firmly, 'I must stress that, on this occasion, I will deal with it in my own way.'

In the following silence Kagan picked a morsel of hamburger from his teeth with a fingernail and examined it closely before putting it on a side plate. 'What do you have in mind?' he said with studied casualness, and Maskelyne replied, 'According to Andre, nature may dispose of the problem for us. Not that I'm relying on that, of course. I'll meet him in a couple of days. And if he goes, we have to head off another appointee, of course . . .'

Kagan asked curiously, 'Why do you think he's a problem?'

Maskelyne looked sharply across at him, but the question appeared to be quite genuine.

'We found out that he was checking up on Sally Kane. That he was getting a little close to the bone with Butterfield. And then there was the trip to Berlin . . .'

Kagan looked at the other man. 'That was your patch, wasn't it? What was his visit all about?'

Maskelyne looked at his plate intently, removing a speck from the side with his finger and wiping it on the linen napkin. 'We never discovered,' he said obliquely, but something in him had hardened. His mind shied from thinking specifically about the problem. I'll consider that later, he told himself.

Driving back through the dusking countryside he cursed

Kalevsky. But, seeing himself with the dispassionate analysis he brought to everything he did, he could not deny his part in the things that had happened. He surprised himself, indulging in a mode of thinking he never normally employed. If only he had never followed up all those years ago, had never hung on, had never felt the urge to revenge, perhaps none of this would have happened. But there was no point. The wheel had come full circle, and he must deal with what lay ahead as best he could.

7

It was Saturday. Maskelyne had risen at six-thirty precisely, as he always did. He went down to the kitchen in his dressing-gown and made himself a cup of strong Indian tea, taking it out on to the terrace outside the french windows. He read his *Times* in a catholic fashion, starting with the sports page. Ronald Atkins had died of a heart attack early on Friday, and he turned to the obituaries column. Poor Ronald. Decent, kind, honourable – and a failure. He had always lacked the iron in the soul needed for success. It had been a little life, after all, for a man whose portions of wealth, breeding and intelligence had been so much greater than the average.

Later, the sun now struggling with a fine mist of clouds, he smiled once, reading the bland reporting of the SALT talks. As always happened, the reporter had fastened on the misleading rhetoric put out by each side to convince their own countrymen that, this time, their negotiators had definitely seen through the deceptions practised by the other side. He yawned and looked at his watch, then stretched his arms into the air.

At seven-thirty the car would arrive with his copy of the confidential report prepared by Senator Reinecke's assistant, detailing the progress of the in camera talks from which all journalists were excluded, as always. This was where the real talking was done, where the all-important numbers were analysed and re-analysed. At the club Kagan had once said to him, 'It's all cosmetics, and both sides know it. Whatever they agree won't change the fact that the remaining weaponry could take out everybody . . .'

By the time the car came up the drive he was already dressed in a tweed jacket, open-necked shirt and grey flannels. He took the case and signed for it, watching the car out of sight round the bend in the drive before returning to his table on the terrace and taking out the sheaf of papers. The sun was stronger now, and a flock of blackbirds pricked to and fro in their pursuit of worms. A magpie flew down, shrieking defiance, but nothing could break George Maskelyne's concentration. He shuffled through the papers until he came to a brown envelope sealed with wax. He took a slim paperknife from his pocket and carefully raised the seal. Brubaker's memo was headed 'Secret and Confidential', underlined. He started to read.

> Notwithstanding the customary biased newspaper reporting giving undue weight to propagandist elements, it seems that real progress might have been made. The 'inner' negotiating team comprises four individuals with their advisers and interpreters. Senator Edward Reinecke, myself assisting. Yuri Ponomarev, with Oleg Grishkin in support. The usual lawyers, counsellors, and interpreters.
>
> Little was achieved in the first week except for ritual gestures. They started by saying that 'a necessary precondition for meaningful discussion' was the removal of the seventy-two Pershings on German soil. We responded by pointing out that these were virtually obsolete, but that it was considered politically necessary to keep them on German soil, as a gesture of American solidarity with the German people. We left this topic unresolved, both sides maintaining their start positions.
>
> Taking the offensive, they then moved on to discuss SDI. On this issue we maintained our usual stance, namely that this was purely defensive and could not be included in a

consideration of 'forward offensive weaponry'. Following on from that our stance during this sector of the discussions was that SDI could form no part of discussions on the European situation. Characteristically, the Russian argument on both these points was pursued at full pitch for the entire week, and was then suddenly dropped. Since they have made no firm statement, but have now turned their attention to the European situation, we are making a guarded assumption that they accept our position on SDI for the moment.

In connection with what has taken place since then we have been apprised via intelligence that Grishkin has been Kalevsky's second-in-command for the past eighteen months. This is an unusual feature, the significance of which we have not yet been able to evaluate.

When we commenced discussion of the European Theatre we took the initiative, pointing out the overwhelming numerical superiority of the Warsaw Pact conventional forces over NATO. Ponomarev refused to discuss this, and made a point of insisting very strongly that 'full disclosure' of all offensive weaponry must be made. Reference was made to alleged use of 'agent yellow' and other chemical and biological agents during the Vietnam conflict, and (a favourite Russian ploy) to the illegality of such usages under various international conventions and protocols. Their negotiating technique is always oblique and they invariably employ indirect approaches rather than direct ones, thus making it extremely difficult to read their true position.

On day four, with all the verifiable UN, American, and Warsaw Pact forward weaponry outlined in papers distributed to both sides for wider consultation and advice, there was a strange incident. The heatwave in Europe has affected us here, and the air conditioning had broken down. By mid afternoon we were all sitting in our shirtsleeves feeling very uncomfortable. The Senator had been insisting again that everything relevant had been disclosed when Grishkin suddenly stood up and started banging on the table. All the previous exchanges had been carried out through interpreters so it was a surprise to find that he spoke perfect English.

Grishkin kept shouting, 'You are withholding information on the British position,' over and over again. We were too surprised to do anything at first, but finally Ponomarev caught him by the arm and pulled him down, saying something to him in Russian. (The interpreter was unable to come up with anything for this exchange.) Following this, Grishkin sat down and Ponomarev then suggested that we postpone further discussions for the day as Comrade Grishkin was unwell. The next day we were told that Grishkin had been taken back home for treatment for 'an incipient heart condition'. (Services are alerted to monitor.) We now have a stone-faced gentleman called Simonov attending, apparently until last year a Supply Minister in the Georgia District.

There has been no more mention of 'the British position', but we have noticed a perceptible softening and willingness to deal in Europe on the part of the Soviets. We will analyse further, in so far as we are able, but it seems possible to suggest cautiously that Enigma has had some success.

Apart from the actual reductions (see Appendix A) and improved methods of inspection (Appendix B) the Soviets have agreed without reciprocity to ban tests for the period of one year. Seen against the intransigent positions adopted during the Brezhnev and Andropov periods, this seems to indicate significant progress.

The remainder of the report contained technical data, setting out the position as at the end of the previous talks, the reductions achieved in terms of numbers of missiles, kilotonnage, range, targets within reach, and annotated (to George's mild irritation) with Brubaker's laconic comments. 'Bullshit. This claim is not verifiable,' he had written alongside one set of figures. George had mentioned Brubaker's flippancy to Kagan once before, but the other man had just said, 'It doesn't mean anything. It's just the way we work . . .' Containing his irritation, George began to write.

He sat at the table until ten o'clock, deliberating over his meeting with Joseph planned for that evening. Half aware, he noted with approval the gardener taking his wheelbarrow full of manure carefully down the path, conscious of his employer's eye upon him. There was a precision to the garden, a sense of order, that George loved, particularly at this time of year. The roses glowed in clumps of red, yellow and white; the immaculate lawn rolled smoothly to its sharp, clearcut edges. The Virginia creeper against the house hung in brilliant golds and reds on the mellowed stone. But his mind was preoccupied and, for once, he was disturbed to find that the clarity and certainty to which he was accustomed had deserted him. Joseph had been there at the beginning of everything that had shaped his subsequent life. That meant more than most things in George's life. And he saw now, with increasing bitterness, the jaws of the trap he had unwittingly devised for himself. It was something he would have avoided, had he been able to see how it could be done with honour. But the only honourable course now was for him to deal with the problem.

He had arranged for the servants to take the night off. That was not unusual, and they had learnt to accept these changes of routine without overt demur. His housekeeper would lay out the cold collation for Joseph and himself on the sideboard before she left. It must be a civilized meeting, he had vowed to himself, despite what had to be done.

He reflected how differently Kagan would have arranged matters. When he had told Kagan about the dinner (to forestall anything which Kagan may have had in mind), the American had been incredulous. 'I don't understand. You invite a guy to dinner and then . . .' His voice trailed off and he shook his head disbelievingly. No, Maskelyne had thought, you'd never understand. So far as he had any real friends, Joseph was one. He and Joseph had been through the war together as a young captain (acting major) and his ADC. They had experienced the deaths of comrades; they had talked of patriotism, honour, love of country, late into nights lit by the flash of guns, shattered by the stuttering artillery of war. If Joseph had changed since then, George could only remember how he once had been. Perhaps, he thought, I have preserved my ideals intact because I have continued to serve. Joseph has lost his because he has strayed into the corrupting world of compromises and botched decisions. (If anyone had ever thought to ask George if he considered himself to be a moral man, he would have said 'Yes', without a further moment's thought.)

He spent the rest of the morning walking round the garden and making a list of tasks for the gardener to carry out the following week. Dead-heading; spraying the aphids on the trees in the orchard; fertilizing the vegetable garden; scarifying and fertilizing the lawn. He wrote these instructions into a black memo book. On Monday his secretary would type them up on the word processor, giving one copy to the gardener, and leaving one copy as a check-list for her employer. The following Saturday he would go round the grounds and tick the items satisfactorily completed off his list. It had taken four years for the system to work to his satisfaction. Now, after nine years, it was almost unnecessary to check, but he did so all the same. Order, method, execution.

After lunch he telephoned the office where Avery was on duty and spoke to him over the scrambler. The instructions he gave were precise, detailed and clear. Nobody listening would have noticed anything unusual in the cadences of his voice. They were as flat and emotionless as always.

But in the afternoon a rare mood of indecision came upon him. Usually on weekend afternoons he worked on his memoirs; that had been the pattern of the past ten years. He had told nobody that he was writing them and he knew, in any event, that they would not be published until years after his death, if at all. But they contained a meticulous record of his observations on the department's successes – and its failures: Blake, Vassall, Bettaney, and the bigger ones.

He slept – normally something he never did during the day – and woke after three hours at five o'clock with a blinding headache. His mouth tasted sour and dry, and his flannels were rumpled. Though he would have to change again for dinner, he went to his wardrobe and put on a fresh pair of flannels. The staff had never seen him in *déshabille*, and appearances must be kept up.

He had his tea and read on the terrace until the sun went down. He took off his glasses and folded them precisely into their leather case. He checked over the cold collation on the sideboard, got a glass of iced mineral water from the fridge, and went out to watch the last light bleeding from the sky and the rooks slowly circling the elms before settling for the night. Then he stood and stretched, and went into the house. Time to change and prepare himself for the evening. It was still warm and he left the french windows open.

8

Joseph had gone round to Elizabeth Atkins' house when he heard the news. She had been dry-eyed and brisk, but he knew that her febrile efficiency, the quick gestures, were quite unlike her: that the time would come when she would weep. Death must have come swiftly out of the morning air. She had gone out to call him in for breakfast, and found him, dead on his back near the folly. 'He seemed to be smiling,' she said doubtfully, looking at Joseph as though afraid he might laugh.

He stayed for lunch. By then he'd gently suggested that she didn't answer every phone call. People would understand. Over lunch the silences grew and he became aware of the growing vacancy in her eyes. They gazed upon some horror that he could not see, beyond his powers to comfort.

He stayed on. She slept in the afternoon and then they had tea together. Yes, Ronald had left everything in order. There were no financial problems, but she would call Joseph if there was anything at all she needed. 'Don't go . . . ' she began to say when he stood up, and then shook her head at herself, 'Of course you must.' When he kissed her she clung hard to him for a second and then said, 'Do you think there is anything . . . afterwards . . . ?' 'Of course,' he lied, smiling at her. She looked very lonely as he drove away.

Ronald's death had brought back the fear. It was so sudden, so unexpected, that it somehow robbed his life of some meaning. Ronald had once said, 'I have been fortunate to have been born with the means to indulge my love of honourable decisions . . . ' and then he had laughed like a schoolboy. 'Doesn't that sound pi? As though such things were of paramount importance . . . ' But they had been, to Ronald.

The next evening Joseph drove himself up the M3. The clouds had gathered during the day and, despite the promising sunset of the previous night, the air was humid and dense. Though the air conditioning in the Daimler was set to maximum, he felt the perspiration coursing down his chest and soaking through his shirt.

There was a pleasure in driving that he had forgotten: it lay in the control over the machine, the instant response as he pressed the accelerator pedal towards the floor. There was a mindless simplicity in going fast, a feeling that one could outrun any problem. Too fast, he thought guiltily, seeing the speedometer hovering around ninety. He eased down with a sigh, and moved over into the middle lane at a sedate sixty-five.

Before starting out he had made two calls. Then he had carefully packed his papers into his battered case. These were only copies. The originals had been lodged in his safe deposit box at Coutts, and another set of copies with an envelope giving instructions in the event of his death was lodged with his own solicitor. As a double precaution he had typed and sealed a letter to the manager at Coutts himself, with another set of instructions that the envelope should only be opened, and the contents acted upon, in the event of his death. All this had seemed mildly melodramatic, even while he was doing it, but then he had reminded himself that he might well die soon from perfectly natural causes. The reflection had made him feel better somehow, as though the instruction was really only a matter of commonsense, after all. Respect for the law had been so woven into the fabric of his being over the years that it was difficult to give credence to his fears; but he knew of some of the things done by the people with whom he now had to deal.

He eased down and took the turning off to Maidenhead. The sky ahead was inky, blue-black, and a warning spray of rain spotted the windscreen. He fed cautiously off the motorway turn into the late local traffic. Incongruously, thinking of George, of the meeting ahead, he found himself recalling Iago's soliloquy. 'Not poppy, nor mandragora, nor all the drowsy syrups of the world, shall ever medicine thee to that sweet sleep, which thou owed' yesterday.' He laughed to himself in quiet amusement. George had removed himself so far from the mundane, everyday commerce of humanity that it was hard to imagine that ordinary considerations, ordinary loyalties, meant anything to him. He took his right hand from the wheel and patted his pocket again. The weight felt strange, not reassuring. Another reminder of a world long ago, when he and George had both been young. It had been reassuring then.

On the narrow country road, four miles or so from Maskelyne's house, a tabby cat suddenly broke from the hedgerow and ran a few paces beside the car. Joseph swerved and braked, but he felt the thump of impact as the car hit the cat. He pulled up on the grass verge and walked round to the front of the car. The offside headlight was broken and smeared with blood. He looked up the road and saw the cat dragging itself in ghastly silence down the shallow ditch which ran alongside the road. Its mouth was open and its small pink tongue lolled out of the side. Its back legs were limp, twisted at a grotesque right angle to the spine. As he walked towards it, a man looked over the hedgerow and observed him silently. A straw-blond stubble fringed a raw-cheeked, chisel-nosed face. The cat lay still as Joseph approached it, looking up at him with blank yellow incurious eyes.

The man above the hedgerow spat at him as he stood over the animal, uncertain for a moment what he should do. 'Bastard. You think you own the road with your big car!' Joseph knelt down and took the cat's head in his right hand, gently holding the body still with the other hand. He twisted sharply, feeling a click under his hand. The body thrashed for a few seconds and then lay still. He picked it up gently and put it on a ledge of earth under the hedgerow, looking at it for a moment as he brushed the earth from his knees. The man screamed 'Bastard!' again, shaking his fist at the sky. Joseph got into his car and drove on.

By Maskelyne's gate the giant, leprous eucalyptus shimmered its leaves in the wind. Joseph nosed the car into the wide skirt of gravel where the drive met the road, and cut the engine. He looked at the clock and saw that he was fifteen minutes early. He opened the glove compartment and took out a bottle of spring water and unscrewed the cap. He wasn't due to take this next pill for four hours yet, but he needed his mind clear of pain and fear until this was over. He put a pill in his mouth and drank straight from the bottle.

The episode with the cat had distanced him, sharpening his mind, and had bleached out the overtones of feeling about what lay ahead. He felt now the calm, judicious certainty of giving advice in the knowledge that his arguments must prevail, because he alone had incontrovertible evidence. He tried to ignore the small voice in his head which would not be stilled. Saying, remember that this is not a court of law. There are no rules of evidence. These men have killed in the past to preserve their interests, and will do so again.

He put the flask in the glove compartment and started the engine.

Carter stood in the door of the duty office, immaculate, watching Avery with a faint smile on his face.

'There's really no need,' he said again, shrugging his shoulders. 'He wants to do the whole thing himself. I can give him a hand with the clearing up.' The telephone rang and Avery picked it up and Carter watched him for a moment before turning round and walking slowly down the corridor.

Rivers came in with a paper mug of coffee and sat down, looking through the papers on the desk. 'What do you think?' he asked when Avery had put the receiver down, and Avery said irritably, 'How the hell should I know? Why doesn't somebody else take a decision for a change?' But he had already put the switchboard through to the nightline and had walked round to pick up his coat from behind the door.

James folded the last letter and put the rubber band round it. He read Lydia's note again, and then put that too at the back of the drawer with Anna's letters. The photograph of Anna taken when they were on honeymoon in Sri Lanka, laughing over her shoulder at him while the cobalt sea stretched to the sky beyond, was next. He took out the note pad and sat down at the desk.

He sat for a while looking at the pad. Then he carefully replaced the leaf he had torn out under the cover, and put the pad back in the drawer.

In the sitting-room he drew the curtains and lit one of the table lamps. At the front door he hesitated for a moment, running through a check-list in his mind. Then he locked the door behind him and walked down the stairs to his car.

9

Tonight George was playing host, showing as much bonhomie as his nature permitted.

'Come in. Come in,' he said, as though Joseph had been coming round to play bridge. Over his shoulder the strains of Elgar came muted from the sitting-room. Immaculate as always, with his silk shirt, old Etonian tie, beautifully cut blazer. He even ventured a touch of playful jocularity. 'Let me guess. Some Château de Beychevelle. Eh?' he gestured Joseph on to the patio and busied himself with preparing the drinks. It was going to be more difficult than he had envisaged, Joseph thought. He sat heavily in the chair, aware already that George was trying to infuse some wartime camaraderie into this meeting, some potent reminder of those shared years.

Joseph sighed. He had observed the same thing happen so often before when he was defending men who, irrespective of what they may have done, felt that their long conversations with him, their intimate confessions, gave them some right to his friendship.

He declined an offer to stroll in the garden in the fading light. George's concern about him seemed to show a touch of ghoulish hope, or was that only imagination? 'You don't look too well,' George said solicitously. 'We'll just sit here and enjoy the garden before dinner.' Other things were out of character, too. He had surprised Joseph by voicing some uncharacteristically indiscreet comments about Kagan. 'I'm sure he's got a lady friend in Geneva. Though what anyone can see in him – particularly with his manners – God knows.' And more in the same vein. Joseph felt, again, some attempt to enlist his sympathy, to underline their similarity, to suggest a bond between them. There was only one way to break it.

He said abruptly, 'Why was that little man – Burberry – sent to Berlin after me?'

Maskelyne said easily, 'The department is concerned about you, Joseph.' He ticked off the names on his fingers. 'David Marsh – dead. Lydia Marsh – dead. Pyotr Alexandrevitch – disappeared.' He paused for a moment, looking at the other man narrowly. 'In fact,' he said, 'we sent two. Bergman went as back-up.'

Before Joseph could collect himself, Maskelyne stood up. 'Dinner's only a cold collation, I'm afraid. I've given the staff the evening off.' He walked through the french windows ahead of Joseph and put on the lights. The music still played in the background, its themes rising and falling. The cherrywood dining-table glowed in the light from the candelabra. Joseph followed, nursing his drink in the crystal goblet. He felt no nearer to finding a way past Maskelyne's defences.

When they were sitting at the table he said carefully, 'So you're suggesting that Burberry's death – the car accident – was just that? An unfortunate accident?'

Maskelyne's face was impassive. He finished chewing a mouthful of food, wiping his face with his linen napkin, and said, 'I'm not quite sure I follow you . . . ?'

'It was Bergman's car that ran into your other man. Burberry was trying to run me down.'

He wasn't quite sure what was worrying George. Maskelyne said that the black Opel was registered in the name of Pavel Slovik. 'The address on the booking form was illegible.' Now his voice carried an unmistakable plea: play the game; there's still a chance that we can keep this from breaking into something irreversible, he seemed to be saying. Aloud, he resumed, 'I can't really believe that . . . but we are, of course, making the appropriate investigations into the matter.'

Sudden thunder cracked viciously, nearly overhead, followed almost immediately by a flickering white flash which lit up the room with a ghastly, oscillating flare, and another loud rumble. Joseph put his hand in his pocket and pulled out the revolver. He put it down by his right hand on the polished table-top, careful not to scratch the glowing surface.

Maskelyne sat back in his chair. His body suddenly seemed rigid. After a moment he said, 'Do you mind if I smoke?' and Joseph gestured his assent. Maskelyne took a cigarette from the silver case on the table by him with his long, pale fingers, and Joseph, still watching him, lifted his briefcase on to the table with his left hand, opened it, took out the yellow folder and placed it in front of him. Outside the storm was growing. Almost a cliché from a bad movie. The rain had begun a sullen, heavy drumming, and the curtains flared into the room.

Joseph had no need to refer to his notes. Everything was as clear in his mind as when he sat in court instructing Counsel. Only here there was no judge, no jurors: and the gun on the table was a reminder of how things really were.

He felt the pain growing in his chest, and made an effort to keep his voice as casual as possible. (Something within him still refused to accept what was happening; even more, what he was doing . . . was saying, these things just do not happen.)

'I wondered from the beginning why you had brought me in, George. There were so many other choices. I came to the conclusion there were three possible answers. The first, which you hinted at in our first meeting when you offered me the Commission, was that you thought I would basically endorse the department's version of events. The second, that I would find the truth, or such approximations to it as were available, but would produce a face-saving whitewash in the national interest. The third, that I would die before my investigations were complete, by which time the affair might have died down sufficiently for the whole inquiry to be quietly shelved . . . ' He paused and looked at Maskelyne, but the other man made no comment.

Joseph sighed and opened the folder, sorting through the papers one-handed. He sensed that the dangerous time was not yet, not while he still had things to tell George, not while George was trying to estimate the scale of the damage and how it could be contained. It would be later, when he came to realize, as he would, that letting Joseph go would bring ruin in its wake. But Joseph had accepted this meeting because he saw no other way of arriving at some truth.

George stubbed out his cigarette and reached for another. Joseph poured himself another brandy. His heart was beating uncomfortably fast, and he willed himself to remain calm. It will soon all be over, one way or another, he said to himself. But still it thumped with the terrifying irregularity, the missed beat.

'There was no difficulty in coming to a view of things. It was absolutely clear from the start that David Marsh would not have committed suicide. I daresay the Sally Kane disclosures were mildly embarrassing, but no more than that, these days. I talked to poor Ronnie Atkins on the phone, two days before he died. He confirmed that Marsh obviously tried to keep matters out of the press, but felt the damage was limited. And he confirmed my own thinking when he said that he thought Marsh's death served some purpose in a wider, covert context . . .' He paused, and took a sip of brandy. Outside the wind had dropped, but the rain continued to patter on the flags by the french windows.

'I concluded that Marsh was disposed of by your people. His wife? Well, there was a problem. Whoever did that wanted it to appear like a badly faked suicide, and to suggest that she had been killed by someone searching for the letter she received from her husband prior to his death. Incidentally, I consulted a graphologist who concluded the note was written by Marsh under pressure. We don't need to speculate how that was achieved, do we, George?'

Maskelyne's hands lay on the table in front of him. He looked at Joseph impassively, even with a slight hint of weariness in his manner. Joseph sighed. Was it really worth all this, he thought. We cannot bring the dead back. But there seemed no other way forward. 'After I examined all the possibilities, dismissed all the parties where no motive was evident, I was forced to one conclusion. That the Russian, Alexandrevitch, was a vital link. Ronnie told me that he had been dispatched to Moscow on a mission. To do with the disarmament talks. That he had disappeared. And it seemed to me most likely that Alexandrevitch had broken under pressure and admitted where his loyalties lay, and that this must be a foreign operation aimed at discrediting the department. After all, on this occasion you had nothing to gain and much to lose from Lydia Marsh's death. The house was under surveillance, and no ordinary burglar would have made it look like suicide, taken nothing, and got away under the nose of the Special Branch. Ronnie told me you had a sleeper, George . . . ' He shook his head, sadly. 'It's a dirty pool you play in, George. Everybody becomes defiled. One of the numerous young men working for you and Kagan isn't quite as straightforward as he seems . . . '

He had Maskelyne's interest now. He resumed, 'About Marsh. I could understand the principle quite well. You have to make genuine sacrifices to convince the other side of the bona fides. Ironically enough, poor Ronnie told me that his retirement had probably saved his life. Otherwise, it might have been him. Well, I don't need to tell you how confused your business is over here at the moment. I couldn't see at all where the ultimate responsibility lay: whose mind conceived the plan, whose finger was on the trigger. Excuse me an old man's bitterness, but the public never realize how circumscribed our so-called 'open brief' is: how many doors are closed, firmly, irrevocably, beyond the reach of the law or of any inquiry. At first my guess-work turned towards Kagan and, just possibly, beyond him to Senator Reinecke. Even before talking to Ronald I assumed there must be a connection with the talks. Who stood to gain most from their appearing to go well? I don't wish to impugn Senator Edward Reinecke's honour, or diminish his concern for the Western Alliance. But my re-searches indicate that he likes to get things done, to have what the Americans call 'a game plan'. I knew, too, that while Kagan has a degree of autonomy he would be liaising with Reinecke over certain matters. Of course, as in all covert operations, the principle of deniability would be para-mount. If the time came and it was fed out through the papers – well, he could always say he didn't know of it. There would be no paperwork to prove otherwise. That is how it's been since Watergate, and the Contra hearings endorsed the value of the approach . . . '

Maskelyne sneered, 'All very interesting, Joseph . . . ' But Joseph held up his hand and said, 'Give me the stage a little longer, George. I haven't quite finished.'

He took another sip of brandy. The pain in his chest had gone, and he felt calm again. 'What threw me at first,' he said, looking down at his notes, 'was that I assumed it must be an entirely American operation. After all, they may not have known of Anna's connection with you – or with James

Bergman.' He smiled briefly. 'I understand that they only used Christian names at Greenham. Anyway, I couldn't postulate a directive coming from our side under the joint arrangement for Bergman to kill his wife and your daughter. That seemed inconceivable to me at first . . . ' He broke off and studied Maskelyne's face curiously. There was a colossal boom of thunder and the lightning flashed again.

Joseph put his hands over the handle of the gun. 'It wasn't,' he said, 'until someone let slip the operation code name Enigma that I finally concluded it must be you. It's the small things that give the game away, George. You can't afford these little private jokes, this sneering laughter at what you see as the stupidity of others. You know how all of us have joked about your obsession with that cheap piece of music with all its tawdry sentiments. And I knew that you had the ruthlessness, the absence of soul, to set this up . . . '

Maskelyne leaned forward into the pool of light from the candelabra. His eyes seemed suddenly alive with hatred, and he spoke with brilliant, uncharacteristic passion.

'You've become just like one of them out there, Joseph,' he said, stabbing his finger in the direction of the garden. 'Obsessed with judicial trivia, unaware of the national interest and all the things we fought our war to preserve. The greatness of our country, the repelling of foreign invaders from our soil, the preservation of our way of life.' He stood up and leaned forward, gripping the table so hard that his knuckles showed white.

'Yes, Joseph,' he almost shouted. 'I did arrange it all. Do you know why? Let me tell you. Anna was the real bishop. But I loved her. You must believe me. True, she had betrayed a great trust, had gone to Greenham Common to try to destroy all that I stand for. But the way I did it puts the matter beyond reasonable doubt as far as the other side are concerned. And as for my son-in-law' – he laughed contemptuously – 'what did he, what could he, know of the sort of sacrifices you and I had suffered? He had to be the instrument of her death. That in itself would reinforce our position. But I also knew that only then could he really understand what sacrifices love of country calls forth. He had to learn that you must set aside all that stands in the way of loving this soil, our freedom, our way of life . . . '

Watching him, Joseph was shaken. George seemed unconscious of any irony in his words. The veins stood out on his neck, and his usually sallow face seemed flushed, fever-bright. He stood for a few moments looking at Joseph and then sat slowly down. If it weren't for what lay under my hand I could believe him, Joseph thought. Could believe that I should falsify the Commission report, could see and value George's ideals, could think truth less important than security, could believe it was hubris to set myself against the wishes of the Establishment in this matter.

The music began again. Looped tape, Joseph thought, distracted for a moment. He shuffled the papers under his hand until the photostat copies from the Berlin Library of Records lay under his hand.

'But it wasn't quite like that, was it, George?' he said wearily. 'You were concerned when I went to Berlin. You must have guessed what I was going to do. You see, I remembered that you had gone back to the trials and had taken up the case of Kalevsky . . . ' He saw the figure at the end of the table stiffen and thought, any time from now it could happen. He moved his hand imperceptibly towards the revolver.

'You remember Honecker?' It was a rhetorical question to which he already knew the answer. 'I asked him to find out a few details about our old friend Kalevsky, via his contacts in East Berlin.' He picked up the paper under his hand. 'All pre-war birth registrations in the territory are conveniently kept in the records office in West Berlin, so I was able to check out what he told me. The beginning, at any rate . . . ' He read from the paper, looking up from time to time to check that George hadn't moved. 'Ludmilla Terreshkova. Born 15.4.31. Warsaw University, 1949 to 1952. Department of Mechanical Sciences. Degree in 1952. Worked 1953 to 1959 at Spolenta Technik Fabricca. Delivered of daughter, Olga. Birth certificate registers "Father unknown". The file which Honecker located in the East is then marked closed, suggesting defection to West Germany.' He looked up over his half glasses at Maskelyne. The Brigadier's face was glistening with perspiration. Despite the storm the heat hung heavily in the room.

'Otto Honecker was able to fill in some gaps for me. Ludmilla lived in a small flat in the Wola district of Warsaw. She was known as a quiet, reserved woman with few friends. An excellent linguist. In August 1958 she met a Russian over on business and – much to her neighbours' surprise – they became lovers almost immediately. He stayed for six months and then left without knowing she was pregnant – until well after Ludmilla had left for the West with her little daughter. Even if Kalevsky was the sort of man to do anything about it, it was too late by then. She had married an Englishman in Berlin, and he had adopted their daughter . . .' Looking at Maskelyne he saw the other man's eyes widen for a moment, looking past Joseph, towards the french windows. Glancing sideways, Joseph saw a movement. There may have been something, but it had gone now. Only the rain poured down remorselessly.

Maskelyne lit a small cigar. He seemed suddenly relaxed, almost bored.

'All right, Joseph. I really must congratulate you. Yes, I married Julia and adopted Anna knowing that she was Kalevsky's daughter. You won't believe me, but it wasn't for spite or revenge. I really loved Julia. Until I discovered she was a sleeper and the whole thing had been rigged. Then there wasn't any question. She had to go. Andre did the certificates. The damage she'd done, right under my nose . . . ' He laughed, exhaling smoke through his nostrils. 'It's the only time in my life I've given way to sentiment and look what happened.'

There was a new confidence in his manner which made Joseph uneasy. It was not the kind of confidence which Joseph had become familiar with over the years. That of a man who has given up and accepted the consequences. It was rather the confidence of the gambler who believes that his luck has changed. He had pushed his chair back and crossed his legs: to a casual observer they might have been two old friends enjoying a post-dinner drink and a discussion of old times. He realized, with a sudden, blinding insight, that the movement he had seen from the corner of his eye must have been one of Maskelyne's men. That there could be no intention of letting him leave this house alive. Too much had been said. But there was still some way to go.

'So Julia was still under Kalevsky's control?'

'Not directly. But you may remember the trouble we had in the early sixties with operatives in the Warsaw Pact countries. Men suddenly being taken in, who were so established they had merged into their surroundings, American businessmen being thrown out of Moscow, all that sort of thing . . . '

'I can't imagine that you would have given Julia any information,' Joseph said, and Maskelyne smiled with acid amusement.

'She was in the milieu. Parties, dinners, conferences. And she had the gift of translating the careless talk people indulge in at parties after a couple of drinks . . . ' His face registered disapproval. 'It was Alexandrevitch who tipped us off. Everything suddenly made sense.'

'So you disposed of Julia. Did Anna know?'

'Who knows what people know,' Maskelyne said sententiously. 'It was one of Kagan's men who did it. She'd had a heart defect for many years. I believe they used amyl nitrate . . . '

Joseph turned his head as the lightning flashed briefly again. There was a darker bulk outside the french windows, sheltered under the eaves. He wondered briefly if he could shoot Maskelyne before he was shot himself, but he had never been much of a shot. As though reading his thoughts, Maskelyne said gently, 'It's no good, old man. In the end we always win.' There was a flatness in the delivery, a sense almost of apology.

Joseph said, 'One last thing, then. The secret that so many have died for, that is so precious, that is going to make a difference in these treaty talks. There is no harm in telling me now . . . ' And, in truth, he felt a great curiosity. The figure in the shadows would only bring the time forward by a little while. Now that he had accepted the shadow into his own life, what matter a few days or weeks more? It would always be ahead at the next bend in the road.

The music swelled in the background. The upper part of Maskelyne's face was now in shadow, so that he seemed to be only a disembodied mouth dropped on to a torso. The mouth smiled, showing teeth for a moment in mirthless amusement.

'Butterfield was in a real panic after you'd been to see him. Demanded to see the Minister, to have a signed quitclaim exonerating him from any responsibility. Your name was mud, I can tell you. The whole orchestra was falling apart, the harmonies disintegrating. Most of all he suddenly suspected that the fat salary might disappear, that all thoughts of a knighthood would fly out of the window. It was pathetic to see him. He never had the facility to work out the precariousness of the whole situation. Even tried to bluster to us about going to the newspapers over the whole thing . . . '

He mused for a while, looking down at his hands. When he resumed, his voice sounded weary, anxious for the whole thing to be finished.

'Haven't you guessed yet, Joseph? You know the situation, after all. CND reviving. The Church getting in on the act. Greenham ladies demonstrating against American missiles on our soil. Labour forced by the TUC into promising a manifesto which offers unconditional nuclear disarmament. Facing the prospect of another assignment to destabilize if Labour got in. You know how asinine all those positions are. But the real threat, which we're just too woolly liberal and polite to articulate, is that neither the Americans nor the Warsaw Pact care that much about Europe. If and when the time came, the special relationship would mean nothing. There is no dual key arrangement. And self-interest could dictate that any Soviet warning first strike would be against Britain, because we carry the can for the Americans, and because we are an island and the damage would be containable. Less likely, when the chips are down, that the others would back us. The lesson would be learned, one way or the other, for the sacrifice of a pawn.'

He lit another cigar, pursing his lips and wiping away a shred of tobacco. Somewhere upstairs a door suddenly banged, and both men looked at each other.

'It's only the wind, Joseph. My housekeeper keeps the windows open. As I was saying, we defined the problem long ago, in the sixties. Public opinion and treaty obligations severely inhibited us in carrying out further nuclear developments unilaterally. There is a curious death wish in the English character. Even after Hitler many of them refuse to understand that the continuance of peace lies in strength, not in pacifism or strong allies. Self-interest is – always has been – the key. So we decided to take advantage of a loophole in the treaty drafts, and look into the possibility of developing something which would fall just outside the technical classification of offensive military weaponry. It could always be justified under a general medical research programme, or fudged as an accidental by-product of some legitimate research.'

He held out his hand and Joseph slid the ship's decanter towards him on its lace mat. Maskelyne poured himself a liberal measure.

'You wouldn't have believed it' – he shook his head in disbelief – 'we had meeting after meeting. Butterfield, a couple of scientific advisers, parliamentary counsel, Marsh, myself. I still remember them with horror. So much discussion about ethics it became like a convocation of ecclesiastics debating Original Sin or the Doctrine of the Trinity. I remember envying Kagan. He has none of those problems . . . ' He paused and looked at Joseph, taking a sip of his drink. 'In the end, ironically enough, it was Marsh who came up with the answer. It was a question of time, of expedience. We had had endless trouble discussing the research area, back and forth, and then Marsh said, "If they believe the propaganda, do we need the substance anyway?" '

Joseph felt sick. All this had been about nothing. Everything was cosmetic, only. He felt a sense of disgust and, mixed with it, sadness at the waste. It was strange, he reflected, how the provenance of an action changed as one delved deeper. In the end it had been David Marsh's profound cynicism which had led to his own death. That, and the fact that George thought, still thought, that Marsh was amoral, expendable.

'So there was nothing at all, then?' he said, shaking his great head in disbelief.

'Not exactly,' George said, in his pedantic fashion. 'Butterfield was working on cellular mutations, spontaneous cellular necrosis, naturally occurring carcinogens. That much was true. But the rest was padding, propaganda. All the dirty tricks one needs in peacetime to prevent war.'

He got up, stretching his arms above his head and yawning. Joseph picked up the gun. Part of his mind observed the wavering barrel with detached wonder. From some part of himself beyond his conscious control he found words of passion whose existence he had never suspected in himself.

'If I let you go there is no court in the land which would find you guilty, or could even try you. But you are guilty. Of murder, of the most basic failure in the duty of care we owe one another. And, though you dress it up in finer sentiments, I can see that Anna's murder was your revenge upon Kalevsky, for the killing of those prisoners, for getting Julia to deceive you.' He raised the gun until the blued barrel was level with Maskelyne's chest. Tears had begun to stream down his face. But George only looked past him and said quietly, 'You're too late, Joseph. Look, my man is here,' and Joseph half turned his head towards the window until he saw Bergman, gun in hand, dripping wet from the rain.

Almost conversationally, Maskelyne said, 'Do it now. That's an order,' and Joseph, looking at Bergman's face, saw the irresolution there. The gun barrel pointed at him and he tensed, waiting for the bullet to tear into his chest. He felt anaesthetized, without fear. Maskelyne said, 'Now,' his voice sharper, more authoritative than before, and Bergman wheeled and fired. Maskelyne stood up, still for a moment, the expression on his face unchanged. Then he opened his mouth as if to speak, and a stream of blood spewed down the front of his shirt and splattered on the polished surface of the table. In slow motion he sat down, and his body relaxed into the chair.

James leaned against the wall for a moment, the gun pointing slackly to the ground. 'We'd better go quickly,' he said, and followed Joseph towards the door. Bergman turned back and looked at Maskelyne for a long moment. Maskelyne's eyes had begun to glaze already, showing the dull opacity of approaching death.

He put out the light.

10

Within a few steps Joseph was soaked. He could just make out Bergman's car, couched against the dark bulk of the hedge.

Behind him Bergman said, 'Get in the car. I'll only be a couple of moments.' Joseph heaved himself into the car, thankful to be out of the rain. He tried to peer out, but the water cascading down the windows made it impossible. He knew now that the papers he had lodged with his bank and his solicitor only told part of the story. He wondered whether any paper could – or would – print what he had to say. That seemed to be the only chance. It was a matter of time now. Beyond George there were men with even less compunction. He had played bridge with them at the club over the years. They smiled easily, dined well, lived in great houses and were beyond the law. They would know much of what had gone on, though George would have kept matters as close as possible.

Beyond the far corner of the house a dull popping sound – then another – came faintly over the rain. He strained his eyes into the night, but could make out nothing beyond the dark bulk of the house, and the massive outline of the oak which stood ten yards from the far rear corner. A figure appeared round the corner of the house, walking with a stiff, unnatural gait. It was Bergman. He opened the door of the car and climbed in. His hair was plastered to his forehead with rain, and Joseph could hear his teeth chattering and could smell a strange, fresh smell which he couldn't place immediately. James turned on the ignition and gunned the engine and they gathered speed down the drive. 'It was Carter, I think,' he said through clenched teeth. 'I didn't stop to look.' He spun the car out of the driveway and into the open road.

Joseph asked, 'Is he dead, too?' and the other man said, 'I hope so. There'll be others of course, but not yet. Our only hope now is the papers. Do you know anyone?'

'No,' Joseph said. It wasn't one of his specialities, knowing trustworthy journalists. What a sheltered life I've led, he thought, bracing his legs against the floor to stabilize himself as the car raced down the rain-slicked road towards the motorway. All he could think of were the law reporters.

Now they were on the motorway. James accelerated and flashed his lights at a Volvo in the fast lane, moving so close to its rear bumper that Joseph found himself pressing his right foot to the floor, bracing himself for a crash. The Volvo driver made a gesture with his finger against his temple as they moved past, and James steadily accelerated to one hundred and thirty. Ahead, the warning signs above the motorway flashed '50' on and off, and Joseph said, 'There may be police about. Take it easy.'

James said, 'There's a man I know who does these sort of reports rather well. A freelance. He has no cause to like the Brigadier . . . ' His voice sounded strange, over-controlled. 'He's someone who used to know Anna well.' His face, lit by the yellow light of the sodium lamps, twisted in a ghastly smile. 'I suppose that may make him a suspect after what we've heard tonight. But what the hell. Even if the *Morning Star* prints it, it will bring the others in as well, give us more time . . . '

Joseph, looking down, noticed a dark patch on James's

shirt for the first time. Now he knew what the strange smell was. On the biscuit-coloured velour seat, a black stain had begun to spread under James's leg. 'You're hurt,' Joseph said, and the other man nodded. 'On jobs like these they score the casing so that the whole thing explodes. It probably looks worse than it is. I'll get us to Fortis Green.'

Released from the pressure to do anything immediately, Joseph was aware of a feeling of confusion. Something in him rebelled at the thought of giving the story to a paper which would exploit elements of it for its own purposes. So many deaths for nothing. Once the story was out, Reinecke would lose any advantage he might have gained. He felt angry: it seemed that George had won, even in death. He could see those bloodless lips sneering, 'I knew you'd see it our way in the end.' Yet if he didn't tell the story, what had his whole life meant anyway? The only way of doing it without jeopardizing the operation would be to geld it, falsify it, withhold the central falsehood which Marsh and Butterfield and George had constructed with such painstaking care. And by doing that he would have colluded, would have perpetuated the lie, would have given the phantasm the benefit of his own honour behind it.

Past Heathrow the traffic was thicker, slower-moving. By now James was breathing heavily, and the patch had now soaked through his trouser leg almost to the knee. Joseph said, 'I think we'd better go to a casualty department . . . '

James laughed shortly. 'It's a bullet wound,' he said. 'The police would arrive in ten minutes and then it would be all over. We'd better think again . . . '

'Then it'll have to be Andre,' Joseph said.

James drove in silence for a minute. Then he said, 'Oh, what the hell. We'll have to take the risk. At least he's still a covert . . . ' His voice was tinged with faint disgust. 'We won't need to worry about him doing anything himself.'

Joseph began to give him directions.

Rivers came upon the body first. Carter had superciliously suggested that he and Avery follow later. 'It's only killing an old man, after all.'

'Here. Here,' he shouted, and Avery trampled through the dripping undergrowth to where Carter lay, propped in a half sitting position against the bole of a tree. He was still conscious, but Avery could see by the light of the torch that he had minutes left, at best. Urgently he said, 'Carter! What happened?' Carter's eyes slowly opened. He seemed unable to focus. His eyes began to close again. Putting his ear almost to the dying man's mouth, Avery heard him say, 'Bergman . . . Brigadier's dead.' 'Shit,' Avery said, getting to his feet and breaking into a run towards the house. Rivers hesitated for a moment, looking down at Carter, and then followed. In the dining-room Maskelyne had slipped sideways in the chair, leaning like a grotesque, broken clown over the arm. Congealed blood crusted on his chin and down the front of his shirt.

In the car Rivers said, 'Where to?' and Avery said shortly, 'London, for the moment.' A little later he said, 'I don't think they'll go to London. There's only one place I think they will almost certainly try.'

At the B312 turning to Feltham they left the motorway. A few minutes later they had skirted Bushey Park and were on their way down to the A3.

11

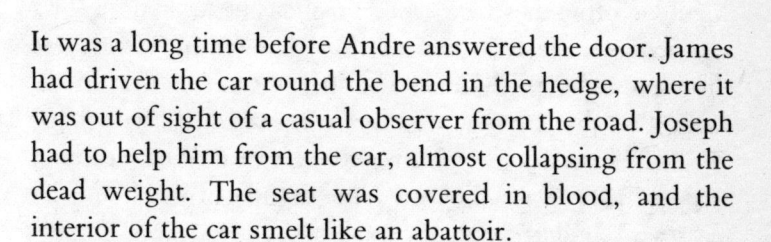

It was a long time before Andre answered the door. James had driven the car round the bend in the hedge, where it was out of sight of a casual observer from the road. Joseph had to help him from the car, almost collapsing from the dead weight. The seat was covered in blood, and the interior of the car smelt like an abattoir.

It was eerily quiet, waiting outside. Eventually a light on the landing clicked on and, through the window beside the front door, Joseph could see Andre coming down the stairs, tying the cord of a burgundy dressing-gown around his middle. Incongruously, he was shocked for a moment at how old Andre looked. He shifted position to prop James more firmly, and waited while the bolts were drawn. The door opened a fraction, still held on the chain, and Andre's face appeared at the crack.

'Andre. It's Joseph. Let us in,' he said, conscious now only of a terrible weariness, and James's inert weight. The door closed again and he heard the rattle of the chain being withdrawn. 'Help me,' he said brusquely, 'he's lost a great deal of blood.'

Together they dragged James across the parquet-floored hall, and into the room that Andre used as a study. Joseph was amused, even now, to see Andre pick up a copy of *The Times* and spread it on the leather seat of the chair before easing James into it. Andre took some scissors from a drawer in the escritoire and began to cut away the blood-soaked shirt. Joseph watched him working for a moment, and then sat down himself in an armchair by the occasional table. He said, 'I know about you and the department. Hans told me you wanted him to keep an eye on me. You were apparently the only person who knew I was going to Berlin. Yet the department knew. But I couldn't believe it until George told me about Julia. You issued the death certificate.'

Andre's fingers still worked busily as he looked up for a moment. He started to speak, but changed his mind. 'He should be in hospital,' he said briskly, looking at the bloody wound on the left side of James's stomach. 'I'll see what I can do.' He gestured over his shoulder towards the cabinet against the far wall. 'There's some brandy, if you like. The glasses are underneath.'

James groaned as Andre began to probe the wound with an instrument taken from the sterile tray he had placed on the desk. Finally he grunted with what might have been satisfaction and dropped something into the kidney dish he had put by its side. He began to put gauze and bandages over the wound. 'We'll put him on the sofa here, and cover him with a blanket. Too much trouble to try to move him.'

When James was settled on the sofa, Andre stood back and gave Joseph an apologetic look. In the light Joseph could see that he had indeed aged; or perhaps it was because he had suddenly been pulled out of bed in the middle of the night. Andre poured himself a brandy, and leaned back against the desk. 'Don't laugh,' he said. 'It was all meant to be a bit of fun, really. You can't imagine how sombre my profession is. Dealing with worried people, with the terminally ill, doling out false reassurances as a specific against *anno domini*. We're human, too. We need some return from life. And, in a Boy's Own Paper way, I thought that my way of staving off ennui had at least the virtue of patriotism . . . ' He held up his hand to fend off Joseph's comments. 'Don't worry. At last, after all these years, I know what it's about now. George told me a few days ago. You can imagine how ashamed I was . . . '

Joseph drained the last of his brandy. He felt a little better now. 'George is dead,' he said, and told Andre briefly what had happened. When he had finished, Andre said, 'I'd offer you a place here, but I think I'll be on the list. Do you know anywhere safe?'

Joseph asked if he could have a wash, and Andre took him upstairs to the bathroom. He washed his face and hands carefully, almost surprised to see the same face as always looking back at him from the mirror above the washbasin. He walked out on to the landing and sat on the *chaise-longue*. Somewhere he felt a sense of urgency, but he said to himself, a minute, just a minute. Looking at the two Impressionist paintings on the wall opposite, the two silk Q'ums over the fitted Wilton, the sympathy he had felt as Andre spoke waned a little. Andre had not done too badly, after all. From the bedroom he heard the sound of Sonya's sleepy questioning and of Andre's staccato replies. Lights from the road flicked briefly across the landing window and were gone. Andre came out on to the landing dressed in grey slacks and a heavy polo-necked sweater. 'Come on,' he said briskly, 'no time to lose.'

In the study he took James's pulse, lifted one eyelid and let it drop. James appeared to be unconscious. 'We can't move him. He'll have to take his chance here. Perhaps being George's son-in-law might save him . . . ' Behind him Joseph said grimly, 'It was he who shot George. Not that they'll know that yet, for sure . . . '

Andre picked up a paper-knife from the desk and knelt down. He levered the knife around a block of flooring and pulled it up. Reaching down into the cavity, grimacing with effort, he brought out an object wrapped in oilcloth, which he undid carefully to reveal a .38 revolver. 'Not you too?' Joseph said incredulously, and Andre nodded, his expression sheepish. 'I joined a club in the sixties. Just attended enough to get this . . .'

He wrote something on a pad and tore off the piece of paper to give to Joseph. 'That's the address of a journalist who feels he owes me a favour. He's done freelance pieces for most of the quality papers. Has quite a reputation. You'd better take my car . . . ' The address was just off Rosslyn Hill. Maybe just over the hour, Joseph thought.

Andre followed him out and pulled the front door closed behind them. Sonya was just walking down the stairs in a pink dressing-gown, her hair in curlers, grumbling to herself. Andre handed Joseph a set of car keys and said wryly, 'Now don't go spoiling my no claims bonus, will you?' He started to walk across the gravel, beaming the garage door open with the control. The shutter began to roll back, and the light came on. The rain had slowed to a fine drizzle. The Bentley looked huge beside the small Renault. Joseph got in and started the engine. As the car began to move down the drive, past Bergman's vehicle, a figure suddenly moved out of the hedge, pointing something at the windscreen with both hands, standing right in the path of the car. Joseph accelerated sharply, and heard a thud. He kept on going. Turning out of the gate and accelerating down the moonlit strand of road he thought he heard a report, and then another. He fought an instinct to go back and see what was happening. The only protection for all of them now was publication.

He decided to take the A3 and passed the roundabout at well over sixty. What a car, he thought, his fear momentarily submerged in the pleasure of driving. It was so silent, so responsive. It was hard to think he was controlling nearly two tons of steel. He felt euphoric, unreal. He turned right at the BMW garage on the A3. In deference to the police station a hundred yards up the road he slowed to forty, and then put his foot down. Passing the Fairmile, he glanced at the speedometer and saw that he was doing a hundred.

He felt young again, marvellously alive. He was going to meet Elaine, and they were driving across to Cambridge for the Pembroke May Ball. Afterwards they would punt down the Cam and watch the sunrise together. Then he would propose. He had thought carefully of what he must say, like a barrister laying out his argument. He would anchor the punt at the water's edge by King's Backs and then kneel in front of her. She would be half asleep, dressed in ethereal white, holding the back of one small hand against her mouth to stifle a yawn. 'Elaine. I am poor, ugly, and of Russian peasant stock. I know that you will probably refuse my request, but I know that nothing is achieved without trying. So I must ask. Will you marry me?' And again, and again, he remembered his surprise, the wild happiness, when she said yes, even looking at him with a wide-eyed, mild surprise that he should doubt it. He had stood there, the pole in his hand, already years ahead, planning their lives together. After a minute she had said, 'You may kiss me if you want,' and he had moved clumsily towards her and fallen off the edge into the river.

Suddenly, in the present again, he saw a white car full of people had begun to edge out of the road from Esher Green. Even with the brakes locked on full he couldn't stop. He saw the face of the girl driving, white with terror, as he wrenched the wheel to the left. The Bentley struck the white car a glancing blow with its offside wing.

The Bentley mounted the grass verge and ploughed into the pine saplings which fringed the dense thicket beyond. The verge dipped sharply from the road, and the car slewed sideways over the scrub grass, slamming its left flank into the undergrowth. It came to rest with its bonnet pointing back towards the road. The engine was still running. Joseph looked over his shoulder at the road behind, half-expecting to see the other car piled against the wooden fence on the other side of the road. But there was no sign of any other car. Ahead of him he saw a light come on, shining through the thicket. Time to go, he thought, feeling again a strange, unreal elation. The gear selector had slipped into neutral and he put it into drive, touching the gas pedal gingerly. The car began to respond, bucking and jolting as the wheels slid on the wet ground at first, then slowly starting to move forward as they gained purchase.

By Roehampton he had stopped looking in the mirror for signs of pursuit. Whatever had happened at Andre's house must have delayed his assailants. What he began to find now, driving the car as fast as he dared towards Albert Bridge, was a return of the unaccustomed sense of uncertainty. A perception had occurred to him which was entirely new – that his insistence on retailing the entire truth might not, after all, be the best course. Was it, he wondered, only a monstrous egotism which made him want to reveal everything, so that no man could lay the charge against his memory that he too had been corrupted? After all, the damage had been done now. Though he had never felt strongly about politics, at least since Oxford, he knew, from long experience with committees, in dusty boardrooms and in government offices, the value of this trump card which he could either deal for or against Senator Reinecke. And, as he drove under the cruel glare of the street lights, he wondered, so near to the end, if he had set too great a value upon truth and integrity. It was ironical that he should feel these things now, with the instrument to make all that had happened known so near his hand.

12

'Christ,' said John Barker, rubbing a hand wearily over his unshaven chin and yawning. He was a tall, laconic man with a tolerant, resigned manner. He had accepted being got out of bed without any apparent sign of irritation, and with a reassuring calm. He had made some coffee, and a sandwich for Joseph, and listened quietly to the story, occasionally interjecting a precise question. Now he switched off the tape recorder and began to walk round the sparsely furnished living-room of his flat, with one hand to his mouth and the other propped against the small of his back.

'You realize that if I can get this printed it would look very bad for the Government? There might even be a vote of no confidence?'

'That had occurred to me. But the more relevant consideration is whether or not a government which authorizes such acts deserves to have the confidence of the electorate.'

Barker grinned, showing yellow teeth. 'I'd agree with you if the other side weren't as bad. They're unrealistic on the defence question, and dishonest about the infiltration of their own ranks by Militant. It is true that the Service has attempted to destabilize them on three occasions when they were in office. It is also true that there has been evidence of Soviet payments to senior officials. Oh, I can assure you that their cupboards rattle just as much, if not more.

Like most villains they shout loud and long at others' villainy . . . '

'Can you get someone to print the story?'

Barker poured himself another coffee and took the percolator over to fill Joseph's cup.

'The problem is getting the right paper to print it. The *Star* would take it like a shot . . . but who'd believe them? The others . . . well . . . you've got a lot of proprietors who would like a seat in the Lords, who don't want to find their next takeover bid referred to the Monopolies Commission. The so-called freedom of the press is a risible misnomer for the expression of the opinions of vested interests. The principle goes through the business, like "Brighton" through a stick of rock . . . ' He sat down and took out a pad. Picked up a pencil and began to tap his teeth. Began to write.

'There is a way,' he said, though his voice seemed to Joseph to lack conviction. 'You'll have to leave it to me completely. It should be possible to get something out within a couple of days . . . '

Joseph felt an enormous sense of relief. He held out his hand and Barker, surprised, took it. 'One last thing. Will you call Andre and find out what happened. Ask him to have his car collected. Tell him . . . I'm sorry about the no claims bonus . . . couldn't be helped.'

He was tired now, too tired to ring Andre, almost too tired to move. There was nothing more he could do. Barker said, 'You'd better lie down, sir,' and he allowed himself to be led into the guest bedroom. He lay down and Barker covered him with a rug, as tenderly as he might a child.

He could hear Barker speaking on the phone. It was difficult to concentrate, but he heard Barker say, 'Everything's all right. They decided to go for containment, stop it there' – and he smiled. That was good. That was good. Now, listening to Barker typing in the living-room, he felt his doubts begin to fade. The sense of security in his own beliefs, the feeling of the rightness of what he was doing, was restored to him. How could he have felt otherwise, he wondered? Whatever had been done the truth should be told, for otherwise history would become only a succession of lies, a false record of specious arguments and incorrect facts. And he felt again confirmed in his belief that there was a morality which transcended all else, which demanded the truth at whatever cost, which in its own way was more ruthless in its disregard of the individual than even George and his masters. He felt more comfortable now, dispossessed of the uneasy feeling that what had concerned him most, after all, was the reputation he would leave behind him. He felt himself slowly drift down into sleep.

His mind went back to that day with George, when they were both young. The shape, the exact texture, the sense of being there which had previously eluded his conscious memory, now returned. The louring black storm clouds against which the shards of splintered walls stood sunlit. He walked behind George, picking his way carefully through the rubble of bricks, the fire-blackened beams, towards the sound of shots behind the ruin of a great wall. Here and there, warming their hands by makeshift fires, mute, incurious men and women watched them apathetically. There was a smell of blood in the air – that fresh, visceral reek which reminded him of his first boxing lesson. Then that scene which he had never really forgotten, only put away in some hidden corner of his mind to deny that men did such things to each other. As he stood with George at the corner of the ruined building, a short man in Russian uniform stood with his gun to the nape of a kneeling man's neck. Behind him a mute platoon of soldiers stood raggedly to attention. The man had turned to look at George and Joseph with a flat, blank gaze, and then fired. The kneeling man had fallen against the wall, his features dragged out of shape as he slipped down, and blood had run wetly down the brick and plasterwork. Two men further down the line of kneeling prisoners had begun to make strange animal noises in their throats. And, remembering it all right to the end, Joseph now recalled that he and George had got drunk that night, in a *Bierkeller* staffed by a cowed man and his wife, and George had said, with a vehemence he had never displayed before or since, 'Whatever it takes, I will pursue him until he pays for this.'

The vision began to fade. He tried to grasp at something – at the shape of what he had done to George, to Andre. But it was too complicated. In the distance he could still hear the tap-tap of the typewriter, but he was walking down a tunnel which led steadily away from the light. He could not see the ground upon which he walked, and there was a strange, sweet smell, like incense upon the air. A few more steps, slowly now, because he was very tired and there was no more light.

13

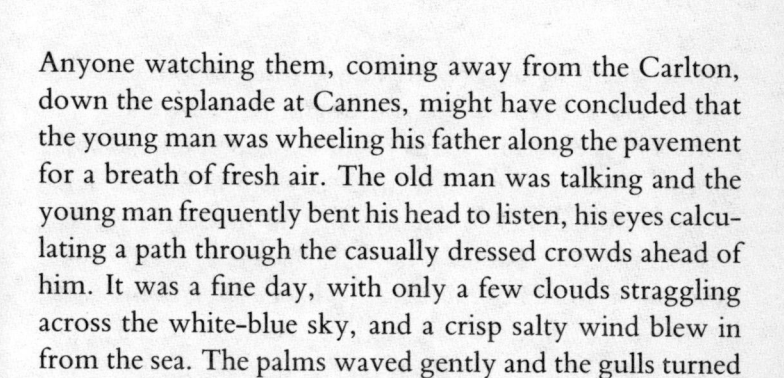

Anyone watching them, coming away from the Carlton, down the esplanade at Cannes, might have concluded that the young man was wheeling his father along the pavement for a breath of fresh air. The old man was talking and the young man frequently bent his head to listen, his eyes calculating a path through the casually dressed crowds ahead of him. It was a fine day, with only a few clouds straggling across the white-blue sky, and a crisp salty wind blew in from the sea. The palms waved gently and the gulls turned and hovered, uttering their desolate, piercing cries.

The older man said, 'We did all we could. If Barker hadn't been under surveillance the *Washington Post* might have received his copy. And I'd known from the start that they would D-notice anything at home.' He sounded quite cheerful, nevertheless.

James Bergman said bitterly, with a young man's anger, 'They always win, don't they? The big battalions.'

'No,' Joseph said. 'People like George might think they had won. But the truth is that everyone loses. And, when all is said and done, one can only be responsible for oneself.'

Nobody paid them any attention as they promenaded down the front, through the jostling, indifferent shoppers.

14

Kagan sat in his office watching a video of the previous week's game between the Bears and the Cowboys. His secretary brought him in his afternoon cup of tea and some chocolate biscuits, putting them down on the occasional table by his side. He'd been in a good mood for the last week now, and, paradoxically, it made her feel uneasy, expecting him at any moment to change back to his dour, grouchy, usual self. 'It can't last,' she confided to the junior in the outer office. 'He'll go on the turn again, you wait and see.' But she decided to put off her search for another job for the moment.

But Kagan's happiness sprang from too deep a spring to be subverted, this time. He felt full of secret self-congratulation, remembering Reinecke's glowing praise on the success of the mission. 'It'll look good in the papers. I'll see you get everything possible out of this,' he had promised. And he had been as good as his word. In six months, after his present term of duty, Kagan was to take up a senior posting in Washington, a prize which would have taken a further ten years to achieve in the normal course of events. To add to his store of contentment, Kagan had in his case a sworn statement from Helga Ulvaeus which he had personally taken from her at the maternity clinic where she had been delivered of a fine baby boy. Of course the Senator would support her, he had assured her. Leave it with him. And he knew, too, that he would be able to call on the Senator for extra favours from time to time.

He'd had a few surprises, as well. He had to congratulate George, posthumously, on a couple of things. The inquest had been hushed up, of course, but the big surprise had been when Sally Kane inherited. When he'd seen her she'd admitted, quite brazenly, that the child was George's. She'd given up the old life now. Become quite respectable. The girl had even been put down for one of the top public schools.

It had been a pity about the waste. The news of Alexandrevitch had come through finally, and the same source had confirmed that Carter was Kalevsky's man. Thinking back to George he tried to be sorry but, in his unofficial moments (such as now, eating his biscuits in his shirtsleeves while he watched the game), he could admit to himself that it was hard to care much, one way or the other. Maskelyne had always been too cold a colleague, and he had always been aware of the sneer behind the official façade.

It was when he thought of James that he felt momentarily uncomfortable. He reached past the cooling cup of tea to pick up a Pepsi, drinking from the bottle and wiping his mouth with the back of his forearm afterwards. He really had thought of James as a son. He had, thank God, resisted Carter's suggestion that Bergman's contract should be terminated. Thinking of it now, knowing that Carter was Kalevsky's man, he felt cold. He had done as much as he could. It had been part of the deal Andre had proposed that night, but he would have done everything possible, even without the pressure. Kagan hadn't been able to sanction the Bureau to continue paying him, but he'd managed to get some money into the account under the heading of 'General disbursements'. Andre had helped, giving evidence in camera to support the view that his wife's death had unhinged James, that he was not fully in command of his faculties. There would even be a small pension, in time. At least he'd managed that. Avery had given evidence, supported by Rivers' statement from hospital, that Carter had taken the Brigadier on Kalevsky's orders, and that they had then taken Carter. That was neat enough. And last week the committee had reluctantly decided not to press for a posthumous honour for George on the grounds that it might provide fuel for 'disagreeable speculation in the press'.

He wondered about James. The boy had moved in with Sir Joseph Sainsbury as some sort of personal assistant cum factotum. He had obviously collaborated on Barker's report, but Avery had managed to track Barker down, D-notice the story, and stop the *Post* getting the copy. It would be much easier to deal with Avery than it had been with Maskelyne. He was a pragmatist. He'd helped to get police cooperation in suppressing information, and that had meant that most of the stories had been killed for lack of authentication. The hints that had got into the paper had been a middle-page, nine-day wonder, which had collapsed from lack of support. Of course he knew that there would always be speculation, and he had passed a few anxious moments himself, but the general perception was that no great damage had been done, and that was what mattered.

Andre had told him that Sir Joseph could only last a couple of months. He wasn't sure that Andre was trustworthy. After all, that was what he had told George originally, all those months ago, but look at what the man had managed to survive. He felt almost sentimental about him. You had to admire a man who had the courage to act like that. Even if he violated your highest ideals by his actions. He shook his head in self-reproach. It wouldn't do to get sentimental.

A rare melancholy memory came to him, without warning. They were dining at the club (where else?) and Kagan had just passed on the news that a mutual acquaintance, a war veteran with an illustrious service record, had been found dead in a brothel. And, to Kagan's surprise, George's words had stuck, over all the intervening years. 'There are no great causes any more. No opportunities for patriotism. Only the filthy paraphernalia of lies and compromises to keep the wreckage together.'

God, Kagan thought, now beginning to get back into the game again. If we all thought like that, where would be the point? But later, after his team had won, after he had dined with Avery and was further reassured that they spoke the same language, after he had mentally cleared his mind of the day's work and was lying on his bed with a bourbon and soda gripped in his spatulate fingers, the melancholy remained. It will pass, he thought, turning out the light.